THE ANGLERFISH COMEDY TROUPE

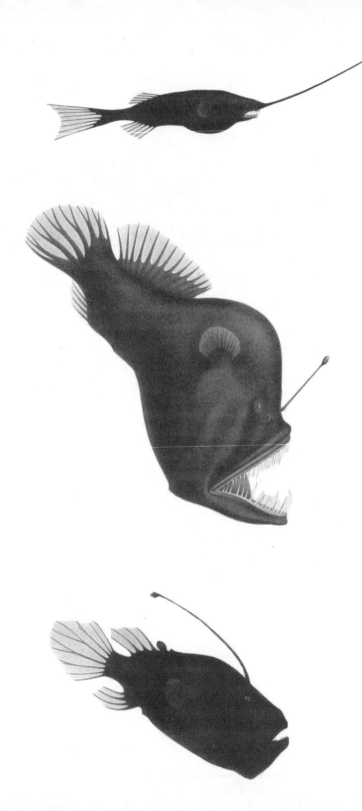

THE ANGLERFISH COMEDY TROUPE

stories from the abyss

COLIN FLEMING

DZANC
BOOKS

DZANC
BOOKS

5220 Dexter Ann Arbor Rd.
Ann Arbor, MI 48103
www.dzancbooks.org

Designed by Steven Seighman

Library of Congress Cataloging-in-Publication Data

Fleming, Colin, 1975-
[Short stories. Selections]
The anglerfish comedy troupe : stories from the abyss / Colin Fleming.—First edition.
    pages ; cm
ISBN 978-1-938103-15-5 (softcover)
I. Title.
PS3606.L4624A6 2015
813'.6—dc23   2015000622

First U.S. Edition: August 2015

Printed in the United States of America

10   9   8   7   6   5   4   3   2   1

Okay, let's do everyone at once, yeah? For Peter Norberg, who goes back longer than anyone with his Dave Kingman swings and falling over on his ass or else jacking one 465 feet; for John Musok, again, who believes—and maybe knows—more than anyone else; for Colin Fleming—yep, you, mate—because you're still alive, which I find gobsmacking; and for Laura Simons, who was nice to me when I needed someone to be. And M: the past was yours, but the future is, well, you know. And the future doesn't stop, does it?

CONTENTS

GREEN WOOD

Every night, in the middle of the night, Doss would turn on the television to what had once been his favorite station and watch the same scene he had seen the night before, and all the night-befores he could remember.

He wasn't sure why any station would play the same program every night, and when he turned on the set an hour or two earlier or later, he always found the same scene playing, no matter what. There was a certain regret in having let his subscription to *TV Guide* lapse, but that had been more his wife's interest than his.

The scene started off well enough. There was a woman, in her bedroom, wearing a flimsy robe as she put on her makeup. You could see her husband behind her in the mirror, wrestling with his tie. They were going somewhere, and even though the tie flustered the man, you had the sense that a pleasing evening was probably in store, one that had been looked forward to for some time.

Just as the man got his tie in place—or, rather, after he had nearly done so, and his wife turned around to help with the final adjustments—the doorbell rang downstairs.

Doss liked this part. The man said, "That will be the pizza guy. Do you have any money? I am out."

The director of the program was very crafty, though, and he had his cameraman cut to the man's back pocket, where the sharp-eyed viewer could make out the top of a twenty-dollar bill. His wife rolled her eyes and reached into the pocket of her robe, revealing the curve of her right buttock in the process and making the man's eyebrows arch.

"Here," she said, producing two tens. "We're going to have to eat fast, if we're not going to be late. You'd think there'd be food at a boat christening."

The man waited a few seconds, like he was thinking, and then said, "Maybe they don't want people to get sick. After all, we'll be at sea. Technically."

This was the one joke of the program, and Doss liked it, as far as late-night jokes went. He was tempted to shut the television off after the man made his joke, but he always hoped he would see something different in the remaining portion of the program—a different resolution to the plot—so he kept watching, looking behind him to see if anyone else had come into the room.

The man went downstairs, to the kitchen, toward the door where he clearly expected the pizza guy. He moved to the kitchen table and picked up a chair, which he put in the middle of the room. Doss was not sure—the viewer was clearly expected to make certain inferences—but he believed that the chair was to be the site of an impromptu romantic encounter between the man and his wife, with the former sitting upon it and the latter pulling up her robe. That's why there'd been that subtly suggestive buttock shot.

But when the man opened the door, there was no pizza guy at all. Instead, he saw another man, with charry teeth, sitting in a wheelchair outside of his detached garage, which faced the door that led into the kitchen. Doss understood this make of house, with no proper back or front door.

There was an awful noise coming from the garage, and, looking past the man in the wheelchair, who seemed to have no hair but rather a blackened scalp, or else a dirty bandana matted upon his head, the man of the house saw an altogether bigger fellow with yellow, rather than charry, teeth and a shirt with cut-off sleeves. He appeared to be destroying the car parked in the detached garage, whose door was half open, and also, for some reason, snapping the boughs of green wood recently clipped from a tree whose branches had been scraping the side of the house, like the arboreal versions of a dozen plectrums. (Doss had had wood like this in his own garage, so he understood without any need for cinematic explanation.)

The man in the program was scared, Doss could tell, but what, really, was there to do in such a situation? You were outnumbered, so there was no sense taking the men on, even if one of them was in a wheelchair. The fellow in the garage was massive and clearly unhinged. The sound of wood exploding and metal popping was overwhelming.

The man, to Doss's thinking, had concluded—as Doss would have—that these vandals would leave soon enough, after they had wrecked everything they wanted to wreck, and then, having studied their appearances so minutely, it would be time to call the police. Better then than now—there was something about this duo that said the worst thing you could do would be to turn your back on them. If you did, maybe everything would go quiet, and you'd walk into another room in your house only to find them in it. Doss shuddered, every night, at this thought.

He watched as the man tried to affect a nonchalant smile, one that said, "Okay, vandals, have your fun, you're not going to frighten me, even though there's nothing I can do about the two of you."

The charry teeth glinted back at the man in the night. The erstwhile noisemaker stepped out into the driveway and stood beside the man in the wheelchair.

The man in the program who looked a little like Doss was still smiling, nodding, trying to project an air of confidence, of mature defiance. The giant without shirt sleeves reached into his pocket, pulled out a gun, and proceeded to shoot the man who looked somewhat like Doss through the head, with the bullet continuing in its trajectory into the kitchen, where the man's wife was now (retrieving the chair) and entering her head as well. And there it stopped.

Doss had already lost his own wife before he started to watch the program, every night. He lost her bit by bit. First he lost her in certain rooms, where he was unable to see her, or tell if she'd been in them. In the rooms where he could see her, it was like seeing ripples, that flash of a person leaving a given space as someone else steps into it, wondering if that flash in the far hallway was a person at all, or just an effect of how the sun had hit the carpet, or a child outside the window waving a toy flag.

When he could only see his wife in corners of every third room, down by the ground, in the interstices of quoin joints—for they lived in a very old house—he still failed to conclude that they were not long for each other, and if cutting away the green wood that had been scraping the house had not provided restorative peace and quiet, it was incumbent upon him to get on the ground himself and venture into those darkling corners, so that he could extend a hand and do his part in getting them back into the center of the room, all of the centers of all of the rooms, upright. But then she was gone altogether, and the nightly episode began to play.

Doss understood he had limited time in the house, but he wasn't sure, exactly, just how limited that time was. Time often overwhelmed Doss, and he remembered how, at the age of five, he had querulously demanded of his father that that particular day couldn't, surely, be the only day that would ever have that name, that timestamp, it would have to come around again sometime, right? Each day couldn't have but one chance to be a day. There was just something too harsh, too implacable, about that.

Maybe it was all of the thinking about time that allowed Doss to compact it, in some sense. He'd go places in his mind, and do things in his mind—places you couldn't go out in the world, doing more things than you could do at once in it. That seemed to help, but it also made him unaware, in most instances, of knowing how much time he had, or even how much had passed.

He sat by the window in the room where he had last seen his wife, down in the corner, on the same side where the green wood had been scratching away at the house before he stacked it in his garage.

A child in a wheelchair rolled past, day after day. He'd stop in front of the window where Doss sat and smiled. Doss noted the somewhat charry teeth, but this was a mere boy. Then again, time was very tricky. And the boy did seem to look older every day, and less boy-like.

Doss glanced around, like maybe events, or portions of them, were starting to reverse themselves. If one of the characters from the television program had gotten young again and was starting over, perhaps he'd see his wife, or some figment of her, standing alone in a corner, and he could get on the ground and try to pull her back up to him.

But when the boy in the wheelchair stopped rolling by in the day, and began to do so at night—such that Doss couldn't tell if he was a boy or a man—and a large fellow with a raggy shirt, its sleeves frayed, began to stand across the way, in front of the neighbors' yard, Doss became concerned.

The television set had long stopped working. Or maybe the cable had been shut off. He didn't remember paying any bills. That wasn't his department. He looked to the quoin joints. Nothing. That night, as he sat in the fireplace, knees to his chest so as to give his wife all of the space in the room if she wanted to return and not feel encumbered or confined, he thought he heard noises coming from his detached garage.

They weren't especially loud, and they might not have been noises at all, but in the morning he wiped the ash off himself and went out to the garage to retrieve the boughs of green wood. There was no car there, for the car had not been his. Still, if it was the boughs they wanted, maybe, when they broke in, they'd take those and leave him alone, and the house would prove more pacifying than the garage had, if the program was any indication.

Truth be told, he wasn't sure if that was the outcome he wanted, or if some plane of his mind was working to find a resolution that would free him from ever looking in the corners of rooms again, down on the ground by the baseboards, for openings in joints, for openings in the past.

He stood the bundles of boughs up and leaned them against each other so that they made a sort of tepee. Inside, he noted that this was more comfortable than the fireplace, even if it afforded his wife less room, were she looking to return, but maybe the fact that he was now totally concealed would help, and there was certainly a curiosity with this new structure in the family room.

Doss did his best to be patient as he listened for noises from outside. In the half-light, he tried to stop up his breath as he watched, at floor level, a wheelchair roll past him. He heard the chair stop, just out of sight, and turn, like it was facing him. But then it turned again, and soon the sound of its tread was gone. Doss waited. When he heard a cascade of feet hitting pavement—light feet, like female feet, maybe—fading off into the distance, he got up and took one last look into the corners of the room.

The man in the wheelchair, and, presumably, his assistant, had replaced the quoins with mirrors. And while Doss was impressed with their handiwork, he enjoyed smashing the glass all the same. Outside, he breathed in the warm air, feeling his lungs get wetter. The detached garage was no longer there, but rather a pile of chopped wood that would probably serve the next residents well, come the winter.

FIRE WITH LEGS

IT WAS FRUSTRATING TO HAVE finally managed to scale one wall inside of the sleep machine only to discover bars on the ceiling.

"Come on. This can't be. I'm not sure I can afford to get much more demoralized."

He gave the bars a shake just to make sure they wouldn't give, but they were as solid as could be.

Someone on the outside must have flipped the dial on his way back down to the ground, because the sounds of tropical breezes gave way to the hum and hush of waves washing up a beach. This, at least, was a relief from the motifs and refrains of the crickets.

Those crickets. A solid eight hours a night, usually. At first, they just went for an hour or two, and then everything would shut down. Not that the inside of the machine ever went dark; there was too much commotion with everyone competing for work. Many of the crickets, in fact, had been ousted from their positions, because it was getting so that anyone could make the cricket sounds.

There were even some bright orange pylons that had no problem handling the requests from the outside for such material, plus a clump of rose bushes, a half-filled salt-shaker, and even a locust that everyone regarded uneasily.

He was a big talker, the locust, claiming that unlike other locusts, which tended to stick together and travel in packs, he'd driven his mates away with the sheer ferocity of his ambition and individuality, given that locusts generally hewed to the company line.

"And you know what that line is?" he'd say to anyone who would listen, which was everyone who got near enough to him, unnerved as they were by his aloneness. "Roam about the countryside, doing the whole plague bit, eating lots of grass. Grass. Freakin' grass. Like that's dignified. So you know what I said? I said, 'Fuck the grass, mates. Anyone can eat grass. A cow can eat grass. But love? Who can eat love?' I mean consume it, just suck it out of someone, yum yum yum. So that's what I decided to focus on. Wrecked a lot of good relationships, locust style. Respect, you know?"

It was a drag hanging out with the locust. He got a lot of work, too. Not because he was an expert sound-maker, but rather because of his intimidating personality. Still, he wasn't anywhere near as versatile as the rock crab. No one got more work than the rock crab. He could do a jungle scene, anything ocean related, or as pure a cricket sound as one could want, and was even a master of fire sounds. All he had to do was procure a tinder bundle—stealing a few leaves from the clump of rose bushes—and rub three of his legs together. Before you knew it, there'd be a spark and, as though the rock crab had some relationship with the world outside of the sleep machine, the dial would be turned, and for the rest of the evening soothing flames would play most everyone to sleep.

After the draining defeat of discovering bars at the top of the machine, he was not anxious to run into the rock crab. The latter, it must be said, was quite full of himself, and you could never trust anything—not fully, anyway—he communicated to you, as the rock crab enjoyed cultivating an image of himself as an enigma. But there he was in the break room, reclining on the fainting couch that had been provided for him, it was said, because of his many talents. As usual, he had a bucket of minnow eyes on either side of him. The rock crab was a glutton, one who reveled in his burgeoning corpulence.

There was little joy in watching the rock crab stuff himself between gigs. Still, one had to eat, keep up one's strength, and given that the entire expanse of the sound machine consisted of but a main stage, a basement where the locust hung out—and engaged in his various modes of saturnalia—and the break room, you had just the one place, really, to take your meals.

No one had ever asked the rock crab why he put the minnow eyes over his own before retrieving them with his pincher claw and popping them into his mouth, but the failure to find a door at the top of the sound machine had had an emboldening effect.

"Look, rock crab—what is it with the eye thing? Why do you need to put their eyes on yours? It's weird. You can't tell it's weird?"

The rock crab, putting the latest pair of eyes back in the bucket, set a very firm gaze.

"There's nothing weird about it. It's quite illuminating, really."

"What is that supposed to mean?"

"When you put someone's eyes over your own, you're able to look into their life. The life they lived. Before the ocular portion of themselves"—there was no disputing that the rock crab was well read—"ended up in buckets such as mine. There's not a lot of range with the minnows. It gets a bit samey. 'Oh, here I am in a tidal pool, isn't the water nice and fresh today, I am grateful for all of this salt, oh look, it's a hermit crab, I think I'll go say hi, he seems to be beckoning me, maybe we have similar interests and could be activity partners, etc.' And then the hermit crab rips him in two. Repetitive. But sometimes you come across something different. Could try it with you, if you like."

"I'm not fully committed to dying. Yet."

"Aren't you?"

"No. Well. I'm not sure. But is there any way to do it without me being dead and in your bucket? I mean, could you maybe just, I don't know, throw me over your face? Like I was a bandana? Or a mask?"

It was then that the rock crab realized his companion had no idea who or what he was.

"You have to be shitting me."

"What?"

"You have no clue what you're doing here, do you? Or even what you are?"

"Well, now that you put it so boldly...I don't. I have a great deal of pain. I know that. I thought about letting myself drop from the top of the box today."

"Wouldn't have mattered. Not with you."

"I suppose I sensed that. Do trains ever come through here? I could put myself in front of a train. Maybe that'd be an effective solution."

"Afraid not. Here. Let me help you out."

Given that he was especially vain, the rock crab always kept a small hand mirror tucked under his armor opposite the three legs he used to make fire.

"Never mind that slime on the side. Being a crab is a war of attrition. You wouldn't understand. But take a look. What do you see?"

"Oh, no."

"Yeah. I thought you knew."

"I had no idea. None. Do you think this is why I'm in so much pain?"

He had figured he looked like a person, albeit one with a different kind of job and special responsibilities, but he looked more like a piece of lightning, maybe two inches in height, that had been snipped out of the sky and made into a little circle, with an extra bit of material—perhaps his head—hanging over the top and dangling toward an empty midsection.

"I look very fiery. Raw."

"Yeah, you do. Still want to try the mask thing? Might give you some insight. It's usually only something I do with dead things, so they're not around for me to tell them what I've seen, but this could be edifying. For both of us. What do you say?"

"I feel like I have nothing to lose."

"Okay, then. Just plop yourself on, I guess."

It was a quick session, because the rock crab was due on the soundstage in ten minutes.

"How was it? Do we have our insight?"

The rock crab was not especially forthcoming in any matters, but he felt bad for the creature standing before him. Plus, this was just good dirt.

"Turns out you were a person—outside the box, that is. First you were there in a house, looked happy, all was good. Like I look when I've done a great bit of work and I have my buckets to look forward to. That's how you looked. And the person with you."

"Oh, no."

"Right. Thought that might happen. Sometimes, with the minnow eyes, they twitch a little after I take them off of my own, like they've become, I don't know, somewhat sentient and pick up on a few things, even though they're not technically alive. My art is a complicated art. You understand.

"And then there was just you in the house. Empty house, save for a tennis ball you kept bouncing against the wall when you weren't grinding your palms together. Or vomiting. Lots of vomiting. That roused the gourmand in me, but I resisted and kept looking."

"You're a good friend."

"Thank you. There must be something about you, sir, that affords someone such as I more clarity than normal. With these minnows, I never get to see what their family members are up to. Maybe a brother or sister is procreating while another sibling is torn in two. But with you, I saw what she was up to. It's almost like...yes. That's it. She's become a part of you. So I guess I was still seeing you, in your earlier form, in a manner of thinking. She wasn't in a house—an apartment. And so much mail! Almost as much as the fan mail I get. Dozens and dozens of letters every week. She'd pick out maybe one in every twenty, for which she'd write checks. The others—one look at the handwriting on the front, and into the garbage they went."

"I can feel all of it now. Again."

"Say—what would you like me to call you? Now that we're going to be neighbors. I'm thinking, technically, you're a shaving. A remnant of something, someone else. Cleaved away. But you're also like a spark, all bright and everything. Want the mirror again?"

"It's okay."

"So, which would you prefer? Shaving or Spark?"

"Spark, I guess."

"And you can call me RC."

"Can I just call you rock crab?"

"It's not like you're going to confuse me with anyone else."

The rock crab was quite vain, but he had also volunteered a decent amount of his valuable time, and no one was flawless.

The cricket sounds certainly were not. How they grated. For as long as anyone could remember, it was cricket sounds, eight hours a night. A versatile virtuoso like the rock crab was becoming bored, drained of his normal verve. Until one day, as he reclined upon his fainting couch, he heard something cricket-ish, but not from the soundstage.

"Spark! Do you not hear that? Come, my fiery friend—put your...well...the side of your fiery self up against the wall of the sound machine. Do you not hear that?"

"I do. There is a cricket on the outside."

"No, you idiot. That is clearly the Mother Crab. Clearly. I would bet my last bucket of minnow eyes on it."

They debated for days exactly what they were hearing.

"There's only one thing to do, then. We go to the outside."

The spark, who was now overwhelmed with memories—which was to say, confusion, having never understood how someone who had become a part of him could forget him like that, make like there had been no union at all, just depart in the night, forever—had been looking for a way to extinguish himself. Maybe a journey with the rock crab would take care of this.

"I thought you said we couldn't get out?"

"I said, as you discovered yourself, there's no getting out through the top. But there's always the plug. And the sound waves. We'll just hop a wave. I mean, look at you—it's like you were born for this. It must have been how you got in."

"How'd you get in?"

"I'm not sure, exactly. There was the basement. I think the locust might have had something to do with it. Greatness doesn't question greatness though, does it? And that's why I'm not going to question why the Mother Crab is sending out a signal for me. That's an honor for any crab, even a crab such as myself. It's RC time, baby! Let's ride that wave!"

The rock crab initiated his latest fire with his legs, and the flames were so close that it was with a certain instinct that they both leapt toward the plug. The spark did not expect to find himself upon a bog, mud oozing all around.

"This is the wave?"

"Of course it's the wave. What did you expect? Not an ocean wave, I hope. The ocean's on the other side of this wave. Oh, meant to tell you. Your old house might be there, too. Sort of seemed that way. But hot damn—let's get going."

Progress was slow for the spark. He found himself clinging more and more to the mud, and he could feel the memories beneath him in the form of detached hands that rotted away as he climbed over the latest thumb, barely submerged in the muck.

The rock crab, meanwhile, danced atop the landscape with a balletic grace that seemed at odds with his corpulence. When a fish darted out of the depths, he'd leap through the air and slash it apart for the sport of it. The spark envied his glee even as he pitied the fish. Some heads landed near where he was crawling, and when he looked in the latest pair of eyes, he saw images from his own past staring back at him. But a mere touch to any severed head was enough to char it and turn it to dust, which he duly consumed, in case he had need of the memory again.

"Well, here we are," the rock crab announced when they came to the shore.

There was an island in the distance with a large, vague form resting supine upon it, and what the spark thought was a huge palm tree looming high overhead. To the west was a block of basalt, but a leap or two away for the rock crab, given his newly discovered agility. A piercing cry came from behind the rock.

"Well, I'm off, mate. That'll be the Mother Crab. Gonna be getting me those candy corns."

"Candy corns?"

"Of course candy corns. What else would you come to the Mother Crab to get? She gives you the corns, you snap them in your claws. You can cut through anything after you get a set of candy corns. Good luck to you."

The spark watched as the rock crab took two giant leaps and surmounted the top of the basalt wall, where he ended up in the mouth—out of which stuck half a dozen minnows and two or three crickets—of an enormous heron. The spark was nearly hit by the shrapnel of the rock crab's body. The air smelled acrid. The water seemed a good place for the spark to extinguish himself, but he was curious what that form was on the island. But how to get there?

Using one of the blown-out legs as a rudder, he sat in the center of the overturned portion of the rock crab's shell. He only had a moth wing for a sail, so the journey took no little time. He thought it odd that he should see the sleep machine first.

She was much larger than the sleep machine, of course. Her head was next to it, and what he had mistaken for a palm tree he knew, instantly, was the shadow that he carried in him, in all his forms, wherever they had been scattered to. The temptation to douse himself in the water was great, but he couldn't help but feel the way he had before about her, and that sizzling sound, and the steam, would surely disturb her rest. So he settled on drifting, instead, for as long as he could stand it.

THE GOD OF NERF

THIS WAS NOT HOW he'd hoped to handle things, but given that the woman who had been his wife had failed to show—which was to be expected—and his sister, too—which was not—and that he already had a paddle and a number of Ping-Pong balls—plastic and Nerf—he figured it was probably best to get started.

He never had learned to serve overhand. His inability to do so was embarrassing when he went on family vacations, as a kid, to the place with the ocean where he would later come to live.

Fishing shacks and tennis courts. So many of each. He was better at casting, but he did that from the side, like the rod was coming out of his hip. He had snagged his sister once. In her overalls. When they were kids. Was that why she wasn't here? Or was it because of all the times he chased her around the yard with a paddle bigger than the one he had now—a proper handball racket—that he used to launch racquet balls at her as she fled, giggling.

He served from the side, too, like a batter batting, but with an uppercut motion like a sidearm pitcher. He tried to imagine himself as one of their ilk, someone like Dan Quisenberry or Kent Tekulve, as he stalked around the room, ready to let his plastic Ping-Pong balls fly.

"Wait. That's risky. Considering we've not done this before. Better to start soft."

Hence, he went with the Nerf balls in his first few attempts. He was surprised how accurate he was. It seemed like every other ball bounced off the forehead of the man in the chair who did not move. Several shots went off the nose, and one "absolute seed" of a serve from the side went right into the mouth and popped out again, a juicy rebound that he knew, for some reason, not to touch.

The figure remained inanimate. The plastic balls fared no better than their Nerf counterparts. This was tiring. It reminded him of weeks in bed as a child. The migraines that led to talks of tumors. Nothing so dramatic. Just migraines, and what he thought of as a lambent, shockingly orange field of pain that shimmered under the lights inside his head, some field of fluorescent crops on loan from a 1950s sci-fi movie. He sat atop a tractor, forcing himself through that orange muck with the air shimmering on all sides of him, like the top of a pool of oil, or the sea way off on the horizon, where even the clouds beg off. Plowing the pain, as he put it, row after row, until the migraine went away. It was an arduous process, requiring many days of concentration, and, likewise, he figured he'd have to get creative with his present situation.

"Look, if we're going to do this, you gotta focus. Because, really, you're going to want to do this right. So, what do we need to remember not to do, above all else, come the...what are we calling it...departure moment? Yes, the departure moment. But the thing to be avoided at all costs is..."

He liked these conversations with himself, in his head. He'd had many conversations that way, even conversations with other people, because he had a strong sense of how they'd respond. But given that he was now alone, perhaps he had overstated these abilities.

"Don't make an athletic move. That's the key, right? No athletic move. No dodging, no dipping, no last-second leaping. We're an athletic person. So it's going to be crucial to resist those impulses. Because you make a last-second athletic move and you're apt to find yourself in, well, a position that will simply be untenable. Still, let's do some prep work. At least reach out to one of M's people. So she can know the state I am in."

M was the person who had been his wife. He did not like to use her full name. She did not know who he was. He wasn't, truth be told, certain that she ever had. He had a theory about memory cards and data-exchange programs that the deities in everyone's midst had control over, and which they swiped into the occasional person as part of this experiment. And anything that got swiped in was bound to get swiped out in time. So that's how he had had a wife who no longer knew who he was, and may not have ever known, and when one is forgotten as though one never existed by someone one cannot forget, one naturally turns to those deities and tries to get one of those new memory cards of their own.

He knew a potential spot. A tidal pool. On a hill. He didn't know how a tidal pool could be so high above the water. But it was a legit tidal pool, not some crag in the rocks filled in by the rainwater, for there were urchins, sea stars, mussels, and a petulant hermit crab of whom he had grown fond.

"Look at him, there he is again," he'd say to his wife. "Isn't he great, way up here in this strange tidal pool, and we're, what, a good two dozen feet above the water and all of the other tidal pools. I wonder if there is anything in nature like this cliff." But his wife never remembered the petulant hermit crab, no matter how many times they saw him.

"You really don't? Nothing? Has someone"—his voice would get very quiet— "swiped out your card?"

Such moments were difficult. He had only recently formulated the memory card theory, and his wife did seem to know who he was, at that juncture, even as she was forgetting so many other things. But if he could get his own data out of himself, he figured the petulant hermit crab—who was, really, more cheeky than petulant, and, probably, a loyalist, after a fashion, given that he never attempted to situate himself in any of the normal tidal pools down by the water's edge—would probably be an apt overseer of the thoughts and feelings he wanted to get out of himself. Maybe he'd enjoy them. This was, he remembered, what the scientists would term a symbiotic relationship. "Like between the sea anemone and the clown fish. And now this hermit crab and me."

But visiting the tidal pool, in the days since he had recourse to take up his paddle and Ping-Pong balls, was not quite like it had been in the past. He didn't get to move as much now. Rather, he was interred in what felt like a drawing a child would make, with Crayola lines and smears on all sides of him, and the hermit crab a reddish blob at the corner of the paper.

This was, he concluded, an inevitable result of having made that cursed athletic move. What was it? Ah, yes. A dip. And a turn. A half pirouette. All of which took his head out of the way, and more than half of his torso. And what had he said? So many times. "Make sure you lead with your head. Headbutt that fucker. Why would you, of all people, be scared of a little thing like speed—or mass—at this point?"

The question was rhetorical, but he was definitely scared. Other solutions were sought. A car. A drive, all the way across the country. Starting from where his house had been, which his wife had also forgotten, and which he tried to dump in the sea by carrying off bits and pieces of it in his mind and sticking his face in the strange tide pool, where the hermit crab gave his cheeks a pinch. But when he came back up, gasping for air, and walked back to where the house had been, he found it was still there, so he'd take a photo and staple it to a postcard, which he'd drop in the mail c/o "M and the god who oversees the memory card project," not knowing that particular fellow's name. But it was such a specific job, someone probably knew whom he was referring to and moved his postcard along the line.

He hoped maybe the ocean on the other side of the country would produce a totally different effect, so when he arrived there he stuck his face in any of a number of tidal pools to see if certain parts of the past could go into what he thought of as nautical storage.

"There's a shitload of room in the ocean," he reasoned, but that second ocean failed him as well. He got homesick for the first one, and he remembered the time, as a kid, when his sister had dared him to drink down a soda bottle full of saltwater. It was a large Fanta bottle. They'd been having a picnic. He sliced his tongue on the edge of a razor clam and thought how much he liked the taste of salt as the blood trickled down his throat. He figured the sea would taste pretty good, too.

The vomiting. There had been lots of that. And so there was again. But as he squirmed on the floor of the public bathhouse, he realized this was more than mere vomiting, as it also brought a migraine like the ones he remembered from long ago, which he hadn't had in years. He felt it all the same. His heart became sharp, like its edges had been filed and now it wanted out of its hold, finally, as if it say, *Fuck you, ribs, fucking tyrants, imprisoners, we're blowing this fucking place.* His vision began to waver and shimmer like those fluorescent crops, and just before the body-consuming totality of the final wretch, he thought, *Yes, this is what it is like, note this moment, not that you'll be able to tell anyone about it. This is what it feels like to die.* And then:

(   )

And then:

(   )

And still more:

(   )

Finally:

"Fuck." Face on the floor. Vomit. Sticky, for some reason. Like it had just been busy trying to coat a candy apple. But something new. A blankness. This was promising. "What am I? Not a what, a who. Okay. But who?" He didn't know. Maybe he was eligible for the memory card swap after all. Everything was bright. That was confusing. The walls of the stall looked like shafts of green light. He tried to put his hand through one of them. Metal. The other wall as well. And the door behind him. He gave it another try.

"Who am I?" Again, nothing. He thought about enjoying himself for a bit, sitting tight. But then there it was. "M." *You have to be shitting me*, he thought, as he remembered every single thing about a person who did not know he had ever existed. And that was before he remembered who he was. When he did, the walls stopped shimmering like shafts of green light, and it was all very humdrum instead. That was when he resolved to get serious about this problem of his.

He was told he had had some kind of stroke. This concerned him only insofar as he did not welcome the prospect of sitting in a room, unable to move, completely locked in place with his thoughts, because he knew those thoughts were such that he would have to get creative—as he did in those times when he took to

his tractor, in his head, to plow those shimmering, fluorescent fields of orange—in order to rouse himself again,
when, really, all he wanted was to be done with it all. So
he had the majority of a conversation with his sister in
his head, saving the last portion of it for an exchange on
the phone.

"Look, if I cock this up, just be discreet, okay? Don't
leave me like that."

And then, it was off to the camping store.

"I'm looking for a temporary domicile."

"You mean a tent. We have lots of tents."

"Yes, well, I guess you could call it that. Do you have a
biodegradable one? So that if you leave it in the woods and
you don't retrieve it, it's not like littering, and it can, you
know, help the soil eventually?"

"You intend to leave it in the woods?"

"There's a reasonable chance it will be left in the
woods."

He assumed it would take some time to get his courage
up near where it needed to be. Inside the tent, he could
smell the sea, and the dirt outside was cut with large
patches of sand. The trains were always on time. Sometimes he stirred, began to get off his haunches, thinking
the improvised approach—that is, opting for a train that
was not the one he had planned on—would make the entire thing more doable.

When he finally made his move, it was because he was
so hungry, and he was tired of eyeing the porcupine that
came by every morning, negotiating with himself whether it would be possible to skull it with a rock and try to
prepare it for a meal.

The train was altogether too frightening, though, and as he made one last plea to the deities who oversaw that memory card enterprise to do for him what they had done for his wife (maybe there was a one-entry-per-family type of thing, he thought, but he and the woman who had been his wife were no longer family, so what was the holdup?), he made the dreaded athletic move back in the direction of the porcupine, who had taken up residence in the tent and for whom all of this must have been very new.

In the first few days of the blackness, before he could see himself again, he debated whether anyone would even try to inform the woman who had been his wife what had happened to him. True, the train had not proved nearly so momentous—as far as the sensory nature of things go— as the episode in the bathhouse stall. He remembered bouncing, and maybe—he wasn't sure—porcupine quills in his face, but his head remained intact, and his memories, too.

He waited for his sister to do what she had to do, discreetly, and had a conversation with her in his head about putting a piece of cloth over his eyes so that it was easier for her, without him looking at her. For some reason, he imagined her stopping up his mouth with balls, lots of Ping-Pong balls, until no more air would come out. But then again, there was that Rolling Stones album cover, a guy with a mouthful of balls, and he was doing just fine, and who was to say that the same would not be true for him?

It was tiring, all of that waiting without being able to see. He hadn't been able to see back when he had the migraines, either, but that was why he'd invented that tractor in his head, something to ride around on, take care of his situation, even though it took a long time to make any progress. That's how he came to discover his paddle, and the plastic and Nerf Ping-Pong balls. Eventually, he mastered the overhand serve, and he rained balls against his forehead, from all corners of his head, from all angles of the room, in an attempt to rouse himself and denounce the deities and their cheap scam. The Nerf balls had an admirable trajectory as they crisscrossed each other in the air, and it occurred to him that maybe if there was a god of forgetting, then he was the god of this. And one god, when you got down to it, probably didn't have need for another.

GENTLE BEN

So: AS IS THE CASE most Sunday nights since I was sent to hell, or at least a kind of hell on earth, I'm in the bar sitting next to the guy who dresses up as Ben Franklin, a.k.a. Gentle Ben. I do entertain the possibility that it's actual hell. I mean, maybe you're not given any official notice. No one owes it to you to send a letter or a form updating you on your status. You're just there. This in turn makes me wonder how I might have died. Renal failure? Blunt trauma to the head? You start to wonder if maybe there's a videotape somewhere down here with your name on it, and maybe you can get the loan of a VCR and rewind your tape and see what went down at the end of your life, at that point when you thought you'd care more than ever, but, because of everything else, you cared less than you would have believed possible, and infinitely less than you cared about her. You just wanted it to be over. "I just want it to be over," you'd say to people, who'd gasp. No no no no no. That's never an option. You can't answer them back. In their way, they are right. But you know now that there are other ways, always other ways, for all things, for more things than you know about, than you'll ever know about. So you don't say anything, but you think the same thing, every time. "Isn't it, though?"

"Over" was a popular word. There was a lot you had to do in connection with it. For instance, you had to accept that it was over. After first thinking that it was over. Prior to hoping that it was not over. And then there was doing everything possible to keep it from being over. You'd tell bad jokes to yourself, in your head, where you started spending more and more of your time, and then all of it, finding it strange that the inside of your head smelled like iodine, hospital gauze, sea kelp, and antiseptic. Bandages. Clean at first, then soiled. "Isn't anyone a fan of under," you'd say, in that bad joke way of yours. "Is there anything I need to get under? Like a limbo pole. Was that what we were like? Limbo. Am I in limbo now? There are no poles in here. Hmmm. Smells cleaner today. Open the wound. That's right. Crack it open and let it breathe. Fumigate. Ah. Ah ah ah."

I know there was a house I sat in for a long time alone. I kicked at shadows—that's how alone I was. There was no furniture, at that point, to impede my foot, so I swung at all of the shadows I saw, really believing that eventually I'd connect with one of them, perhaps knock down a wall when the fucker ricocheted. That's how shadows are when there's no furniture and no one else but you in a room, and the next room, and the room after that, unless a burglar has gained ingress, but you imagine the preponderance of shadows would put off even his ilk. The back window was useful. A nice view. The birdbath and the little platform screwed into the garage, supporting a corncob jammed through a nail so the squirrel you believed had come to recognize you on sight had his own dining station. The cardinals and jays were reliable too, and the mourning dove, who only ever came after dusk, when the shadows had retreated to the corners, more or less, to rest up for tomorrow's encounter. After all, there were only so many tomorrows left, and then you would never be there again. They would remain, though. They would have…what is it that shadows have when they are left to themselves, unresolved…ah. Yes. The run of the place. Just like they have the run of you.

Anyway, it's usually just me and Gentle Ben at the bar that I think is probably in hell. He typically has this rolled-up wad of cash on him, about the size of a muffin. No clue, until tonight, how he comes by it. A bunch of teetering women happen into the bar, causing Gentle Ben to bust out his American flag-covered umbrella, stand up, and adjust his pantaloons. The women all wanted a photo. They all get one, at two bucks a pop, never mind that they look like ghosts to me, each with the same face, that face that went into the shadows that melted into the corners of all of those rooms once the mourning dove turned up.

Teetering women depart into the night, and I swear, it's like you can watch them blow away as the breeze picks up. Gentle Ben turns to me and shrugs. I shrug back, thinking, you know, no one would be surprised if they were sitting in the audience at a play set in hell. We don't usually talk, Gentle Ben and I. Gentle Ben and Me. There was actually a Disney short in the 1950s called *Ben and Me*. I used to love watching it. We've not discussed that either.

But tonight I told him I dug his autobiography, and maybe he should think about doing another volume, documenting his latter-day adventures, or at least pitch someone on the idea. And he says to me, "Do you know anyone in the business? Think I could get an agent?" Fairly certain at this point that I am in hell, I tell him that my cock recently entered the business, to which Gentle Ben says, "A toast to you, sir." We clink our glasses, and silence resumes.

THE UNBOUND MARKER

HE WAS AN ADMIRABLE MIX of shale and slate at his bottom, which gave him a nice base and helped him grip the earth. Not that he was particularly pleased with this base of his, solid as it was. Or so it seemed, before the great undertaking commenced.

He suspected he was no different from any other marker that hovered over a mass of flesh in that, over time, he hoped to learn to lean at a rakish angle, such that the trees on all sides, with their emphasis on growing as straight as possible, would regard him with a proper degree of mystery and respect, like here was somebody who could teach everyone in the forest something new.

It wasn't often he had the opportunity to teach anyone anything new. He didn't even have any other markers with which to communicate. There was just him, as far as vertical structures went, and the trees, but no one else, of course, was rectilinear.

The trees were dark like he was, their leaves devolved into shades of blue and purple that had a knack for looking black even in the middle of the day, when the sun made its token effort to extend some rays all the way to the forest floor. But the trees rarely conveyed anything at all, unless severely pressed. Some of the snakes, like the black racers, could impel the trees to hold forth, but that required a good deal of climbing, and a good deal of regurgitating, usually of frogs. For the local trees apparently had a great aversion to frogs, and the marker would wonder why this was so, and do his best to put the matter to one of the black racers whenever he came along to slide up the marker's back and take a rest at the top portion of him, which was not made of shale and slate.

He knew he was a hybrid. The sandstone that was his crown made him less pure than other markers, he presumed. But who was to say? He had never seen any. Efforts had been made to inquire whether the trees had ever known any of his fellows, and, if so, where those fellows had gone, but there was an endemic of black racers in those years, it was believed, and while one did not often encounter the snakes, this was put down to their crafty ways and ability to blend in with the darkness, which was general, or at least much more common than the light, given that the forest had grown unchecked for so long. The trees did their best to look out for each other, shedding their leaves as early as possible each year so as to deprive the racers of the cover deemed so essential to their tree-climbing and frog-regurgitating schemes.

"Idiots," one the racers—in fact, he may have been the only one, as no one had yet spotted two racers in the same place—volunteered as he flicked his tongue against the top of the marker, a faint aroma of mouse and grackle emanating from his mouth.

The marker did not mind the racer. He was chattier than anyone else, and the racer had proved most edifying in the past, when the marker first realized that he was more tree-like—in that he was adept at processing lots of information—than, strictly speaking, slate and shale and sandstone-like.

"And why do you think that is?" the racer asked as he lazily lounged on his back, trying to pick the odd dragon-fly out of the air. His jaws moved so swiftly that the marker could barely see them, and, naturally, he felt envious, and tried to move himself at his base, but considering that he couldn't even lean at a rakish angle, there was no way he was going to get anywhere.

"I don't know. All this time being here by myself, I guess. Well, not by myself, as in all alone. You know what I mean. There's you. The trees." The racer chomped down on a wayward bumblebee and spat its head capsule in the direction of some cedars and sumacs. "That beaver who comes up from the pond to piss on me sometimes. The birds you eat. The frogs. Plus all the things you tell me about that I've yet to meet. That fish that doesn't fit in the water."

The racer was a bit of a cad, and, like many cads, he struggled to keep his various stories straight, but he could usually count on his audience filling him in.

"Fish that wouldn't fit in the water? Hmmm. Fancy a bit of stinger? I could just spit it out on your top here. No? Very well. But the fish…"

"The one whose jaws are like yours, you said, but wider than the circumference of the lake, so that he has to put his head on the beach, and you walk into his head, and then he takes you. It's dark, there are spikes—what did you call them? teeth—on the top and the bottom..."

"Oh, you mean the cave fish. Yeah. He'll fuck you up. You're lucky you live up here. Although, I bet he'd dig a little guy like you. You'd probably have to give him what's under you, though. As a token of respect."

"You mean my flesh?"

"Yeah. You'd have to cough up the flesh. Want me to burrow down there and see how it's doing?"

The marker did not want to offend the racer, but he knew that while the latter was, for the most part, good-hearted and inspiringly articulate, he also couldn't help himself when there was something to be consumed. He would overindulge and grow corpulent every few months, but then the marker, who never slept, would see the racer early in the morning, before even the trees were active, moving as fast as he could from one edge of the forest to the other and back again, and forcing himself up large boulders for hours at a time, until he was back to his streamlined self. At which point he became a paragon of rapidity—that is, you'd be going about your daily business, and boom, it was as if he manifested himself in front of you, a winning grin on his blackened lips, which were sometimes daubed in blood, the occasional mouse hair or splinter of jay beak a sort of de facto accessory. The racer liked to cut a dashing figure.

"So you really don't know, then?" the racer repeated, in his singsong way, his tongue flicking against the marker's top.

"It seems like I should, the way you put it…"

"Think about it, man. It's a piece of piss. What's different about your top?"

"Well, it's more porous than it used to be. But that's a given when we're talking sandstone and an ocean climate."

"All the salt in the air."

"Yes. All the salt in the air. And then I guess there were the lichens, but I don't see them anymore, do you, racer?"

"No, marker. And why do you think that is?"

The answer unfolded brilliantly, just as the moon did every evening over that particular forest, where the sun had so little effect.

"Yes! The lichens got inside my top, and they've grown and grown, and how could I have failed to become a capable thinker? With all that organic matter. Why, not as capable as yourself, of course…" The racer belched and spit up a bit of wasp wing on his left eye before his protective membrane had a chance to snap shut, but he pretended that this did not sting at all. "…but capable enough. But why am I here by myself? I mean, why is there no one else like me? You said you've been here for a long time, right? Forever, wasn't that it?"

"Four forevers, actually. That's even longer than the cave fish, if you do the math."

The racer's nonchalance regarding the topic of his longevity was most impressive, and the marker worried he was not worthy of the snake's company. He felt some of the flesh beneath him. It had grown hard over the years, and grainy. But he could still tell what was flesh and what was clay and sand.

"What are you doing?"

There was not much the racer failed to notice, especially when he had his tongue on the ground, as he did now. The marker hadn't even been aware that his friend—if he should be so bold—had moved, but this was one of those times when the racer was in prime shape.

"Just checking. I like to feel like I'm in..."

"Accordance? With yourself? Yeah. I get that. I could go down there, if you like. Check things out. As a friend. I wouldn't say anything to anyone. It'd be between us."

"No. I mean, no thanks. I'm good. For now. I can let you know if things change." The marker knew, of course, that the millipede was the ideal individual for such a job, but the millipede had met an untimely end.

"Is this about the millipede, then? Because I'll fucking tell you, marker, if you were training in this forest, sprinting as best you could from side to side, and you saw this fat tosser out there every day, blindly—no, let's call it what it was—stupidly crashing into everything and yukking it up with the trees, you'd have done just what I did."

"Bit him in two and left just enough of his top so he bled out on the ground for four days with no one to help him?"

"Fuck yeah. These things happen. This isn't productive. It's not what I'm looking to do with my morning. I'm gonna go shed. You think about my offer."

The marker felt he had caused the racer grave offense. He wished he had a beetle to make a peace offering, or, better still, a frog, but no frogs ever came to visit him. Maybe he could ask the beaver about it.

"I'm sorry..."

But the racer had shifted his focus, and the marker looked down to see him licking his shale and slate base.

"Has that beaver been pissing on you?"

"Of course. I'm the youngest thing in the forest, so it makes sense. Pecking order."

The racer smiled his winning smile.

"That's cute. We'll hang tomorrow. And keep an eye out for that new pheasant for me. I have it on good authority that one of his legs is fucked up. So, naturally, I'd like to try and kill him. Even if he is a bit out of my weight class."

The racer did not keep his appointment, and enough time passed—and how lonely it was—that the marker despaired of ever seeing him again. The trees must have known something, because every single one of them—from the wiriest birch to the thickest spruce—swayed more than they ever had before in the breeze. And everyone knows that trees do not sway in that gentle, rocking way of theirs unless they have some reason to be relieved of their ever-present anxieties and can feel their confidence growing.

Soon, they sent out missives to apprise everyone of their status. Naturally, some of these broadsides blew up against the marker, and what he read in the veins of each leaf—the texts were very consistent—troubled him.

The racer had had a falling-out with himself, it was reported, and, given that no one else had ever been in

accordance with him (the marker felt he had been slighted on this point), the beast was utterly alone. The notion
that someone could have a falling-out with themselves
made the marker shudder, a rare feat considering his constitution. As a result of his pronounced isolation, the racer was being hunted by every living entity in the forest.
Those were the rules: no one could be totally alone. You
had to respect at least a verisimilitude of rank and file.
There were reports, in more leaf-based dispatches, that
the racer had attempted to consume himself (to no avail)
and spent his evenings racing across the forest floor,
but not so fast that a fisher cat, or a raccoon, or even
one of the dimwitted possums couldn't pick him off. He
launched himself out of trees, who were now happy to
have him in their branches, knowing full well his inten-
tions, but he always had a way of landing—even when he
came down squarely on his head—such that he remained,
more or less, intact, the only telltale sign of trauma being
the lines of blood in his eyes as a result of shorn vessels
and veins.

The marker kept a lookout for his friend, thinking
maybe he could shepherd him back to himself, but he never saw him. Maybe, he hoped, this was a matter of the racer not wanting to implicate him, somehow, in the entire
scandal, a testimony to their bond.

The racer never stopped, according to the reports,
and had lately taken to the pond where the cave monster
was said to dwell in an attempt to get himself gobbled up
by trout, or snipped into little pieces by the crayfish and
snapping turtles. Indeed, he would lose parts of himself,
but the bits would grow back, and the racer, to his con-

fusion, found himself more…well…how could he put it… racer-ish than before.

Still, there were perks to the racer's absence. The marker discovered memories he was not aware he possessed. Most of them had to do with the flesh beneath him. He didn't know exactly to whom it belonged, or if he had acquired some kind of squatter's rights and he was the rightful owner of what remained, but he did have a sense of hustle and bustle, of people—yes, that's what they were—around him. He never saw people now. But there had once been people, and they lived on all sides of him, amongst the trees, with their dogs that later became wolves. Or like wolves. That was after the people left and their dogs stayed behind, becoming feral, part of the forest.

What a shock it was—and how he remembered it now—when, a long time later, someone returned in the middle of the night, when the marker was always at his most alert, to hunch before him on bended knee with an arm stretched out to his top, where the salt air had eaten away the stone and the lichen had gotten in the holes, so that he could think as well, he expected, as a marker ever had.

The marker, of course, did not know what this meant. He saw two glinting red eyes looking at him from the edge of the darkest part of the forest, but even if it was the racer, he could not trouble the snake for his opinion. He had enough burdens of his own.

The marker thought about the man for a few days, just as he thought about the racer. He worked to accept that he would probably never know the significance of the flesh buried beneath him. He tried to bond with it, and shifted his weight a little, almost like he was caressing the top of the bone he could feel jutting up near his shale and slate base, but his efforts only went so far.

He busied himself, instead, with reading the dispatches from the trees, pulling for his friend to fall back into favor with himself, or, that failing, to remain unconsumed, for he really believed that was what the snake wanted, despite his efforts to the contrary.

He was glad the racer had respected the one great forest proviso of someone who was at odds with himself, and that was that all attempts at communication were forbidden. So it was with a great degree of consternation that the marker looked down at his base one morning to find a piece of snakeskin with a great deal of text, so far as snakeskin writings went, present in the various striations and grooves that crisscrossed each panel of former flesh.

"Marker, my friend. If I may be so bold. Don't be a douche. I write this in haste, for I am laboring to strike a deal with the cave monster that will grant me relief from my trials, and, more to the point, set me up as the top dog—you know what I mean—in the forest. The fun thing about falling out of favor with yourself—not that I wish it to happen to you—is that when you get back in, so to speak, you get to see what a cool fuck you could have been all along, minus a few missteps (or, in snake par-lance, mis-slides). Only, you're more humble. Granted, I might not sound especially so now, but you know how it is; you shed, you get new skin, you're a bit of a dick for a few days until the novelty wears off. As for what's underneath you…okay. I admit. The millipede told me before I bit him in two. Like I said, I wasn't the best guy in the past.

But what's underneath you is nothing. You're ceremonial, mate. For all the people who died here and got buried who knows where. I thought you should know. And when you're ceremonial, you naturally get shipped about. That flesh is in your head. Best of luck in your new digs. Don't sweat getting dug up. I'm sure it doesn't hurt as much as you think it does. Cheers, B. Racer."

The marker was overwhelmed. Was he trying to be cryptic? Probably not. The racer was always a straight shooter, no matter what you thought about him. Even the trees would probably grant as much, if pressed, which was easy enough to do with a tree.

But just as the marker resolved to settle into a period of deep thought, evaluating the racer's words, he heard a great din on the side of the forest where the cedars and sumacs were, a sound akin to a thousand pieces of bark splintering at once. But this was not the sound of the thresher. It was the sound of everyone's reaction to the sight of the racer, his head frayed at the neck, dangling out of a hole in one of the cedars where a rabid chipmunk sometimes lived, when he wasn't out on one of his debauches.

The next day, the man who had once knelt atop him returned to the marker with other men, and they cleaved him from the ground, put him in the back of a flat-bed truck, and drove with him away from the forest to another coastal town, where he sat in a cemetery, among fancier-looking markers, for many years before he was again dug up and transferred to another coastal town. There he sat atop a cliff, the lone stone once again, symbolizing something—he wasn't sure what—and looking out to the sea in the direction where the cedars and sumacs had once been, where now stood twin lighthouses on their own private island.

Without anyone to talk to, he despaired, and he wished he could send himself over the cliff, but even if he had gotten better at moving around (he wasn't sure how much was due to the men who transported him and how much to his own burgeoning ambulatory skills), he had been weighted down with a heavy plaque that made mention of all of the people who had once lived in the forest where he had once lived, who had been lost at sea, presumably this sea he now looked out upon.

"What are you marking, marker? Time? Ha. That's an old one. I've just had an ocean dip myself. Got some hard-line negotiations going on with some of the big brass down there. Gonna fuck that saltwater shit up."

"Racer?"

But there was never an answer to that simple query, no matter how many times the marker thought he heard his old friend—and may well have, such was the racer's unique tone of voice and ability to become himself again—as he looked out over the harbor in the direction of the twin lighthouses and their red pinpricks of light that made even the local fireflies jealous.

ÉCLAIRS IN THE ANNEX

HE WAS HESITANT TO RETURN to school after being away for so long, but he had reason to believe it would be different this time, especially now that he had sent off the required paperwork to deal with the matter down the hall. There was no sense in preoccupation with the latter, he told himself, and quoted a friend's remark on hearing that he had filed his paperwork and was hopeful the saga with the room down the hall was now at an end.

"You can only control what you can control," the friend had said, which seemed obvious enough. "And not even that, all of the time." He was one of those friends who liked to follow good advice with a tart line that was supposed to be humorous, but then again, the friend had never had a room down the hall that had caused him so much trouble, taken so much time, drained so much energy, and incited such fear and confusion as this room had.

This friend, naturally, would not be going back to school, although he was there to see him off, waving from the curb as the bus departed that first day. It was most important to retain the proper details in this return to school. As he remembered leaving on a bus, a long time ago, he wished to depart in one again.

The friend indulged him in the waving, just as he had finally acquiesced, "Here you are telling me again about this situation you have down the hall. I cannot believe, after having been friends with you so long, that you would lie one thousand or more times about anything. Lie somewhat, and for some time, yes. But as you have now made more than one thousand statements on the subject, I can only conclude there must be some truth in what you say. Or that you believe what you say you've seen. That doesn't mean I'll see it, or that it was even there to see. But let's go. I'm ready now. Show me what you think you're seeing."

The bus ride in was uneventful, even as he fretted that he'd walk into a situation that confirmed his latest nightmares, where he was the only student in a building that had no exit, or he kept forgetting the combination on his locker, or he missed classes he didn't know he was registered for. In other words, the normal kind of thing.

Being the only student at the school didn't trouble him, for he had the run of the place, although, to his credit, he never did run, even though the empty hallways practically called out to him to race up and down them, run laps around each floor. He did wonder how many laps would make a mile, because he was able to run three, outside, and it was only natural that he'd get curious inside and wonder if he could manage the same distance, or whether he'd get dizzy, considering how many turns he'd have to make.

As it worked out, he could not remember the combination on his locker, and he had the sense that his locker was being moved on him anyway, like some days it was on the third floor, other days the first, and even sometimes in the annex. He didn't care for the annex. It was smaller than the rest of the school, and there was little room for running. There was little room even for walking, the walls being so close together. The faster he tried to walk in the annex, the more he scraped himself up against those walls, and he did not have a practical solution to this predicament, or an explanation for the physics of the thing. This brought him back to the matter of the door and the room down the hall; so maybe it was for the best, having this new puzzle to work through.

He remembered someone telling him that the harder something is, the more beyond you it is, and the harder you work to figure it out, the more you progress as a person, even though—or because—you're never going to understand the thing fully.

That person told him this was character, but when he shared the anecdote with his friend, the one who had finally agreed to see what was down the end of the hallway, the friend spat, as was his custom, and made a joke about women and breasts that was quite sexist, but meant, it seemed, to say something like, "That's a loser's mentality. You're better than that."

As he left the annex, where so much concentrated thought was required, he did allow himself—he felt guilty about it later—to wonder if only a loser would stop with the breasts, if he'd been invited—or given the theoretical opportunity, anyway—to, as his friend put it, "frig that old ginny hole."

It was a long first day and a tiring first week. The weekend was not so much rejuvenating as forty-eight hours spent in stupor, head under the covers, telling himself that he was finally being kind enough to his body to allow it to catch up on its sleep, but knowing, really, that he was in bed with the door shut because of the situation with the room down the hall.

Actually, it felt, being in bed, as if he were in the annex, where everything became much more concentrated, and it was almost impossible to think about the things that had once brought a certain amount of leisure and levity to his life, whether that be his friend's not especially funny jokes that he couldn't say to women, the ball games he watched on television, or the éclair he sometimes got from the bakery as a special treat. But the éclair way of thinking and the annex way of thinking were very different.

Come Monday morning, there he was again, fighting the urge to run around the empty school and trying to do the kind of thinking that was honest, studious, committed—in other words, the sort of thinking that was expected of you in the narrow corridors of the annex.

Maybe then he wouldn't have to go there—or, better still, wouldn't be scared of going there, and could dispense with his fears in general as he became someone who simply dealt with things, viewing whatever happened to him, or was going to happen to him, as a problem to be solved, nothing to weep over, nothing to cause him to shake or make plans with himself that he always put farther and farther and farther out into the future. He told his friend about this.

"So what you do is, you say, 'On the first of the month, I'm going to start dealing with this issue. I'll be organized by then, in my thoughts, and my room will be clean, no clutter anywhere. And then I just deal with the issue. Whether it pertains to the situation with the door and the room down the hall, or anything else. Oh—and I'll stop drinking too, and then I'll get thinner.' That's the gist of it?"

It was.

"I don't know, man. Live your life like a thrown knife. That's what I always say. Move on."

This made him sad. Even if his friend did live life like a thrown knife, it was doubtlessly easier to do so when life was ball games, éclairs, and jokes that were funny when you heard them and less funny when you thought about them. Whereas he had other business to attend to, for the simple reason that he had been made such that he was unable to forget.

He'd be sitting there, or sleeping there—it did not matter—and, all of a sudden, an entire conversation from years ago would return, verbatim, and he could see the exact shapes of hands, fingers, nails as they moved through the air, the way one strand of hair, and then two, fell against the mouth; the one crack in the lip, at the top right, that would be gone by the next conversation, which was remembered in the same degree of detail. And the words, of course. His own, plus the ones that came back to him. The volume, the lack of volume, the syllables that fell on top of each other like drunken, ravenous, comically out-of-shape dogs.

He was a good student, though, and his attendance record was perfect. At the end of the semester, he was rewarded for all of this with his own berth on the bus. The berth was not overly large, but it was comfortable, and it afforded him some privacy after his long days in the annex, struggling, but maybe—maybe—getting a little closer to understanding what he could never fully understand.

He told his friend about the berth, and how it was the one thing he looked forward to every day, that gave him some respite, which caused his friend to say that "berth" sounded like a lot of beer, or, taking a great sniff of the air, "beer, wine, rum, cheap whiskey." Again, one of those jokes.

But he must have been making some progress, because eventually he was comfortable leaving the door to his berth open on his ride home, and he wasn't even startled when, one day, a woman with short black hair and compact muscular legs—a cross between a pixie and a soccer player—introduced herself as Margaret.

"Can I call you Maggie?" he asked.

She said no. He worried that she knew there had been a Molly, and maybe about the situation with the door and the room at the end of the hallway, but that means she'd been spying on him. Still, people on school buses are fond of gossip, so who knows what she had heard. When she asked him his name, right before they became an item, he said, "Laird." He used to be one of those people who wished to be known by a single name, like they didn't have a first one or a last one, just this kind of identity stamp. She asked if she could call him Larry, and he said yes, that would work too, but in his mind he thought of himself as Laird.

His friend was happy for him, and happier still when he saw a photo. "Wow, dude. She is smokin'. Like a little fairy gymnast. Or a gynegist, if you get my meaning."

He didn't, but figured this was the latest in a series of gynecological jokes, most of which were punctuated with a punch line about a speculum, a strong sedative, and a high-def camera, for the friend was a doctor, and even doctors have fantasies, which go a long way toward making sure they don't try to enact the plots of any of their jokes.

When matters became amorous, he tried to maintain his distance, but she kept pressing the issue in the berth, in her various states of undress, nipples protruding almost like thrown daggers paused in midair, or captured in flight by a skilled photographer.

"We can't," he would say. "We mustn't."

She laughed, thinking he was making a joke in which he adopted a chivalrous aspect and did a funny little voice, as if he were a knight just stepped off a horse and this was a standard bit of his. "And why mustn't we, Sir Knight?"

"Because I'm very potent," he'd say. "So you need to be okay with abortions, I guess, because it's still so early for us. In the meanwhile, we can just use our mouths. I'll start, if you like." And he kissed her up and down her side, at the narrowest part of her rib cage, until she fell asleep, and then they were on better, more understanding, terms.

He knew he wasn't adroit in giving much of himself, and matters were lax enough that they'd sit on a table, he in his normal clothes, she without any, and people like his sister took next to no notice of her, like on the day his sister came into the room talking about how she and her girlfriends had formed a band, and the first stupid name they had come up with had given way to another stupid name that was, at least, shorter, and maybe for that reason more memorable. His mother would drop in too, and when Margaret said hello—for she was always polite— she'd get back, at best, a harried wave of the hand.

"Your mother doesn't like me," Margaret said, her body so white and clean, like someone had taken a blade and carved her out of an enormous block of soap.

"It's not so much that," he replied, rubbing his hand along the underside of one of her arches, or else across the back of her neck. "She simply thinks it's too soon. And I'm not ready."

"Is it because of the situation with the room at the end of the hall?" She saw the look of fear on his face before she had come to the end of her question. "Your friend, that kindly doctor, told me, right before he tried to lighten everything up with a joke."

"Was it the one about the woman who screams out for the doctor to kiss her, and the doctor says no, it's bad enough that he's already fucking her?"

"Yes, that was the joke."

"I see. That means he trusts you."

"He thinks we should take turns, he and I, watching with you. Outside the door. At the end of the hallway. I can start, if you'd like."

He gave this some thought, some real annex-style thought, where there was no room for running and one scraped against the walls.

"Okay."

Margaret opened the door to the room where they'd been sitting, but only a foot or so. That was plenty of room to look all the way down the hall, where there was a door that was more or less transparent, but with streaks of wood fiber in it, so that it had a kind of dirty translucency. They watched as a man imprisoned a woman in what seemed to be an enormous building—"It's like a castle," Margaret remarked—but was really just a two-thousand-square-foot house that existed on the other side of an un-openable door. The man did various beastly things with some real medieval overtones to them. "Is that Mary?" Margaret asked.

"Yes."

"And that's…"

He looked away from her for a few seconds, and then tried to be brave. "Yes."

When Margaret left, to be replaced by his friend, he worried he'd never see her again. As his friend watched the door and the room at the end of the hallway, the jokes stopped, the éclairs he had brought along were thrown away, the television playing the ball game was shut off. And they watched.

The days at school were spent entirely in the annex, with none of his classes scheduled back inside the big building. Because there had been no way to enter the room at the end of the hallway, and yet it was clear that the room held a certain amount of dominion, it had been necessary in the first place to write a letter and push it under the door, seeking permission to return to school, to study history and various branches of the social sciences. No answer had come, but neither had permission been denied, and he took this to be clearance of a sort. But now, as he watched the woman stuck behind that door, subjected to so much, he knew he'd have to initiate a vigorous letter-writing campaign on her behalf.

Margaret watched while he composed and composed as the light began to leave the house, and it was just the two of them, with no visits from his music-making sister, his on-the-go mother, or his friend, although they spoke to him often enough on the telephone when his friend got bored at his office or his latest patient was due to be waking up.

One letter after another was stuffed under the door, which became less and less translucent by the day. He had a hard time making out where it was, and the hallway was losing its shape, too.

"Come," Margaret said, standing up and taking his hand. "Come." They walked to where he was fairly certain the door was and stopped. He put his hand out, feeling nothing. "Come," Margaret said for the last time as they walked through the space, out into the night.

"*We mustn't*," she said, doing quite a convincing imitation of what she had taken for an imitation of his. "Well, I say we must, Sir Knight."

He thanked her and began to cry, thinking maybe he'd try to call his friend Slit Man, as he had before—at his friend's bequest, of course. But in the meantime, even as he lay in bed, it seemed better to suggest the procuring of a couple of éclairs.

"What are you talking about? It's three in the morning. Are you doing jokes?"

He allowed that he was, and let her press up closer against him.

RED TIDE

No one was sure what became of the water. It had been there so long, in vast quantities, and it had a habit of gobbling up all of the land that it could. This was welcomed, even feted, as a big feature of the town, so far as the tourist trade went, with the water maintaining its knack for being decorous in human/ocean matters.

If you had a house on the shore, you didn't have to worry about it going anywhere, it was said, although Doss, at least, wondered how true this was. He made quite a spectacle of himself when he did his wondering, as doing so involved yelling at great volume to his wife, who would nod every now and then, and sometimes run around Doss's back to get on his other side, so that one ear was not made to suffer more than the other.

It was a challenge not to watch Doss when he got to yelling. You couldn't tell what, exactly, he was saying, but each continuous sound, which probably was a word, seemed quite extended, so one gathered that Doss had an enviable vocabulary, if not one that worked well at high volumes.

There was talk of asking his wife if this were true, as though she alone understood what this great, questing, questioning man was saying, but the other wives of the town thought this would be indelicate and overreaching. Or so they reported, officially, to their husbands, who spent their time at the water's edge, asking questions of their own. The water would never answer, but it was concluded that such was the nature of dialogue with an ocean, and if you did not keep up your end you could not expect to have your house spared, perhaps, on the next occasion when the sea skulked inland in the middle of the night. It had no problem devouring churches, bandstands, shops, pubs, meeting halls, fishermen's lodges, gazebos, and a silo, but houses were left intact with generous swaths of solid ground on all sides. You lost your driveway, but a dinghy would solve the problem of how to visit your neighbor, and considering what the sea could have done to you, everything seemed fair enough. Livable.

But Doss wasn't having it. There was no way he was going to acquiesce, as his neighbors did, no matter how decorous or consistent the sea was. He ordered his wife outside with one roll of paper towels after another, and later drop cloths, to try and blot up all the moisture while he watched from what had once been the bedroom window, high at the front of the house, which Doss had lately fashioned into something akin to a captain's quarterdeck, framed in glass.

It was there that he watched, one morning, as the sea rose in all directions around his wife. She didn't fight it, because, really, what good would that have done? She did wave back toward Doss as she opened her mouth and drank deep. The moment she did, Doss lost sight of her, even though the water remained, and contorted itself into a column that went straight up, straight out of the harbor, over many of the surrounding houses, and right to Doss's makeshift quarterdeck.

He could feel the glass growing hot, which was surprising, given the brackish, bluish-green water that danced only feet in front of him. He saw his wife, and he spat, and out she came, back into the yard, without her drop cloths, which angered Doss, as he hated to be wasteful.

No one saw Doss's wife for a time. But that was probably because Doss was immersed in a venture he thought would make his name, not only as a singular individual but as an artist who could command nature itself.

Everyone knew the sea was implacable. The sea knew it better than anyone. Some of the town's residents, when they were in their cups, late at night, in the basements of the homes that had been converted into bars (to make up for the absence of proper bars), would grumble, in whispers, about the ocean's arrogance, like it thought it was better than they were.

The wives were more conciliatory in these matters, and would generally tell their husbands that, well, the sea was the sea, so maybe it was on to something. Weeping would ensue, for it was hard to have life dictated to you, and by something wet, and without a voice that you could ever really hear, save in the sound of waves resonating off the rocks. Still, you learn to accept your lot, for this is what life is, and it was said that the men of that particular town loved their wives more than men did anywhere else, where wives were less conciliatory and less in accordance with what the sea had to say, in its quiet, understated way.

It was not known if this was true of Doss's wife, but it was presumed. After all, she never stopped listening to her husband, even when the volume drove the on-lookers away. There was decent sport in watching Doss froth and fume, and wagers were shouted from house to house across an expanse of sea, whether his heart would give out, or if the sea, which had been so consistent in every matter, would finally declare, *Enough, this stops here*, and send up a mighty wave to pluck the iconoclast from his driveway and carry him off somewhere else, wherever the silos, gazebos, and meeting halls were now.

Everyone knew that you couldn't expect the sea, after all those years, to break tradition, but Doss set to work nonetheless with an ax. Over the course of weeks, he chopped at his house from every which side as the sea, and the town, looked on. The sea was positively gobsmacked. It was so mesmerized by this performance it produced no waves. Doss's wife was not to be seen, but everyone, save the sea, all but forgot Doss had one, such was his intensity and concentration of rage.

Splinters flew from his ax as if it were a buzz saw. The wood, which had been white, began, deep in the process, to turn red and wet, like it had become saturated in blood. The gulls, who were normally big blood fans—they loved nothing better as a beverage, whether from the carcass of a seal or from one of the corpses of their fallen fellows—stayed away from Doss's yard; this was too much, and no one could tell if this was real blood or something tainted, the result of some inward state made external, in which case you didn't want to be drinking it.

Even the sea was confused. The men sensed this, and nodded sagely to their wives to suggest that everyone and everything was fallible, after all, and consulted its smartest lamprey—one of those oracle types—on the matter. The eventual report was grave, very grave indeed.

One had the feeling that the project would never end. The residents of the town tried to stay awake throughout the ordeal, but one can only hold out for so long. Husbands and wives floated, asleep, in dinghies tethered to their front doors, undisturbed by the sound of ax on wood. The sea had no need for sleep, and it sat, ever watchful, with Doss's wife.

She had used a water-based saline treatment for her ears, and now heard her husband properly for the first time as she lay in the crest of a wave that the sea occasionally caused to rise above its surface, just to keep up appearances. The privileges that accompanied its rank could, in such a scenario, be withdrawn, and the sea had no interest in being downgraded to a lake, a pond, or worse, a puddle. It had come too far. And, what's more, it had finally figured out how to do things that no sea ever had, and while its techniques had been controversial at first, there was no arguing with the results, save in the case of Doss and his wife.

The latter, too, had succumbed to sleep when Doss started to pitch the splinters of his home into the sea. She had not slept in as long as she could remember, even when she had slept in the traditional sense. All of the long days, running around her husband's back, changing ears, had the effect of making her feel like she had been awake forever, or as near to forever as she could imagine. She doubted her imagination on this point, though, and when she once asked her husband what he thought, he roared, and that was as clear an answer as she could have gotten, even if no one else knew exactly what Doss had said.

The sea kept the crest of the wave holding Doss's wife out of harm's way as the splinters, beams, and sticks came flying her way. The process went on for days, weeks, months; it was hard to say. There had been a lot of chopping, and the pieces of red-colored wood were all very fine, like needles, or shards of asbestos, or a splinter's splinter's splinter.

Finally, when the last bit of house had been thrown into the sea, Doss, too, gave in to sleep. The affair was exhausting, having taken all of his considerable strength and will. But when everyone finally reconvened, and even that most trusted—and busiest—of the sea's lampreys, who had myriad consultations to attend to, had turned up to see how the drama unfolded, there was great confusion.

The sea, it appeared, had devoured Doss's house, even if it had been force-fed. This was the accepted outcome, and Doss, pleased with himself that he had done what no man thought possible, forgot, for a time, about the joy he had once derived, long ago, from his wife, before he forced her to go around his back, to switch ears. His yard was very dry, and given that his house was no longer upon it, he had plenty of room to lie down and stretch out in the sun and dream deep, dream the days away, while his neighbors awkwardly paddled their dinghies to and fro.

But lying about in his yard with the sea at bay did not suit him as much as he had expected it to. All the less so when he thought he caught sight of someone who might have been his wife in the crest of a wave, like she'd been tucked away in there for safekeeping. The waves would crash against the land, and each time he heard the sound, he'd reach for his wife, remembering how he had once had one.

Eventually, the sea determined that enough was enough, and retreated back toward the east, leaving a sticky salt marsh behind.

There was grumbling in the town for a time, as the tourist trade suffered, but the marsh turned out to be a wonder. One visiting conchologist after another remarked about the unforgettable sight of the man, an amateur in these matters, who picked up every last clam he came upon and gave it the most questioning of looks before breaking it open atop a rock.

Not a lot of joy was to be had in watching him desperately pick through the pieces, but whenever a conchologist advised that it was oysters that made pearls, rather than clams, the man would speak in the most lucid terms, and his tale of what he was looking for was such that screams would have been preferred, but it was far, far too late for that.

LAST WATER

ONCE HE HAD REALIZED what the noise was, there was some debate, of the internal variety, over which room to go to first. He opted to start upstairs, first venturing into the master bedroom and shutting off the faucet and the bath there, then making his way down the hallway, to the half bath, before returning downstairs to shut off the kitchen sink.

The thinking was that maybe the water was overflowing upstairs, and if he didn't start there, it wouldn't matter what he'd done with the taps on the ground floor, if the ceiling had caved in and there was water everywhere anyway.

He recalled, later, thinking it was cute that his wife had left in such a fashion. She was bound to at some point, as he realized, and all in all it was nice to avoid a scene and not have to expend all that energy yelling. His doctor was most insistent on the point of his stress and blood pressure, and yelling was not a boon to either.

His habit of leaving the tap dripping was one that displeased his wife greatly, although there were a number of his habits that slotted into that category.

She was not especially a fan of irony, the person who had been his wife, so he perfectly understood the statement she made when she married a man who did the same thing he did—which is to say, he worked on a boat. The two men knew each other in that brusque way that men do who work on different boats but depart from the same harbor.

His wife had complained for years about the nature of his job, working at sea, and the attendant dangers, and what that bespoke for them, so he bristled, at first, that she took up with a man who did what he did, as if to say, "It wasn't the job I objected to, but rather you, as a person. The job was a handy excuse. How I wish I could have seen your face when you heard that water rushing everywhere and knew I was gone."

He actually liked the sound of the water, at first. When he had a quick errand to do—like when he had to untangle the knotted fishing lines in the small backyard—he'd leave the kitchen sink running, because the rushing sound proved pleasing upon coming back inside, and this suggested to him that he was not so easily played or influenced.

But that was before he began watching an infomercial, late at night, which seemed to play just about every night. His life was the same in one sense, in that he lived where he had before, and he did the same job that he had before, although he had come to despise it in a way he once would not have thought possible. He did not run the water anymore when he uncombed the knotted fishing line in the backyard, and would even apply packs of cotton gauze to the underside of the taps to try and ensure they were as dry as possible.

In the morning, he'd put his hand to the gauze and feel moisture, and he'd practically reel. The infomercial was soothing, though, in that part of its thrust was that you, no matter who you were, could have more control than you probably had in your regular life, in that you could be Laird, Lady, or Lord of your own land. You could make whatever rules you pleased, and if someone entered your land, it was because you had granted them the right to, and they could no more leave on the taps than they could dispose of you or replace you with someone else, let alone someone far more careless and dangerous than the man with whom his wife had replaced him.

At first he thought the man who narrated the infomercial was Irish, because of his funny accent. But it wasn't right to stereotype people like that, so he tried to pay more attention (the infomercials came on quite late, when he was groggy and looking forward to sleep, which was the thing he looked forward to the most, or, really, the only thing he looked forward to). He learned the man who talked about being master of your own land, for not much money at all, was Scottish, and you should come to Scotland. One's land could be a single square foot or one hundred square feet, and that was enough to make you a Laird, Lady, or Lord.

The idea of being a Lord seemed a little pompous, so he began to think about being a Laird. He went to the library—after stopping up the taps with cotton gauze—to research what this meant, and what Scotland was like.

He hoped it would be quite dry, and when he learned that it was not—and in fact was the opposite—he became desperate, and researched dryer climes where he might be able to be a Laird without having to sacrifice what had become his principles. He took a leave from his job, much to the captain's surprise—for he was what was known as a lifer, there like the dock's attaché, a man who went from boat to boat doing what he could.

He did not wish to fly, nor drive, so he mapped out a bus course to get where he was going. The sailor in him, accustomed to rocky seas and to what sometimes had to be done in them, thought about inquiring if the bus driver ever felt he had to lash himself to the wheel, just to keep going, but looking around on the bus—and this was but the first one—he detected a certain uneasiness in the passengers, and it was important that the crew never alarm their guests. He wasn't crew in the strict sense, but since there was only the driver on that side of the ledger, he wondered if he might be called on in a tricky situation.

The fifteenth bus let him off at a tiny weigh station in a place unlike any he had ever been. The ground was made of dirt, but it was firm like granite, and the air was dry and thin. He inhaled deeply, and his nose, so used to the smell of brine, was stung by the scent of sulfur and peyote in the air. He walked up the road to a house that was more like a shack and knocked on the door.

"Are you the guy here about the land? Er, the parcel?"

He said he was.

"So you're Laird? Is that your first name or your last name?"

It didn't matter, so he said it was just what everyone called him. The woman pointed in the direction he was supposed to walk. "Ten miles. Out that way. Toward that saddle on the horizon. A hundred square feet, just as you wanted."

He thanked her and began to walk toward the saddle. The voice was loud behind him.

"Mister, you're gonna want to get some water first. Get some water here. This is last water."

She went inside, presumably to get some, but by the time she came back he had already dunked himself in the trough the horses drank from, soaking his clothes, and was starting to feel them getting coarse again in the heat. He thought of how some sailors never get dry again, not really, and how an ocean is most unlike a lake, in personal matters, in that one can be dredged, and the other cannot.

When he came back, three days later, after the end of his first reign as Laird, he found the woman sitting on her porch, drinking from a gallon bottle of water with one more next to her.

"I told you it was last water. What did you think last water meant?"

He took a drink and splashed his eyes, thinking it could mean a lot of things but knowing what she meant, even if it were not possible that she could know what he meant. So he took her up on her offer of supper and resolved to reclaim his land in the morning, in one direction or the other, even if that meant turning on a tap or carting a few bottles with him.

THE CHAR PAPER
BLUES BAND

THEY WERE THE TYPE of band, over time, that could play just about any kind of gig you could imagine: wedding, supper club, football stadium, birthday party, Christmas morning brunch, open-air pavilion, museum, right down to the back seat of a car. Not that there wasn't some controversy in coming up with a name that stuck.

"For the last time, we're going with Char Paper Blues Band. I appreciate the sentiment of the Dissolution Unit, and the Demolition Unit has a similar feel, but again: they're both misleading. We're not doing the dissolving or the demolitioning, are we?"

Silence. Initially. Stafford was used to it. The harmonica player would probably grumble for a few days over having failed, yet again, to rename them.

Stafford didn't mind the silence; it was frequently remarked, by Stafford, anyway, that silence was central to their sound. Or ambient noise, at least. The rush of wind in the trees, the blur of cars passing by a house—the dull rattle of a soda can rolling across pavement, the scratchy scudding of a wad of sandwich wrapper passing down an alley. For that was how the band traveled, undetected. This was regretful, because what does a true artist want more than recognition?

"Impact," Stafford would say, when the harmonica player, who was known as HP—the Char Paper Blues Band being a most hip outfit—bemoaned the band's lack of national, or even regional, acclaim. But there were all sorts of bands in the world, and some bands had to be the kind that went undetected, with a cumulative ego so small, despite HP's ambition, that you couldn't see the band at all, even if you wanted to, even if they were on a top label that spared no expense in marketing.

There were other bands that made their way from gig to gig on the back of the wind or a clump of newspaper—more bands, Stafford reckoned, than anyone knew. His father had been a stave, and he was proud of his lineage, and proud, too, of his name, even when his bandmates razzed him a bit the day they made their way to the latest gig atop the mud flaps of a flatbed truck that was, in fact, a Chevy and not a Ford, although the point of the joke was still understood. Camaraderie was useful, in their line of work. Stafford's chief responsibility, besides being the group's leader, and, he felt, its conscience, was in marshaling everyone into playing their parts, difficult as they often were.

HP, it must be said, was a virtuoso. His sound was crucial to anything the band undertook, and his talents were so extreme that Stafford, when the situations in which they performed became oppressively bleak, would allow his star musician to extemporize rather than stick to the planned charts and arrangements. The piano player—the steady P Squared—the bassist extraordinaire—who went by BE, which doubled as a command and his chief directive for anyone who asked him the key to life—and the master drummer—who was originally MD, but became, as one would expect, Doc—could blow up a storm. And they had plenty of reason to when they finally got their gig as the busiest of house bands.

For years, they struggled, waiting for the call. The day jobs were a grind. Stafford hired himself out on fishing boats, doing his part to create the sound of stray waves making louder reverberations against the boat. He had a miniature piano for that. And if he was small, the piano was ridiculously so. Occasionally, a mackerel—but only the tiniest of mackerels—would make its way up to the surface to have a look at the boat's motor, where Stafford generally did his work, but if the mackerels ever saw him, none had any interest in doing him harm. Perhaps that was because he frequently gigged, during these downtimes, with HP, and HP did mackerel sounds better than mackerels themselves, so when they heard how pleasing they were, a degree of ego entered the equation, and life became more about wondering if a calling had somehow been missed and whether it was too late to do something about it. Those were nice bonding moments for Stafford and HP, who would share a laugh that sounded like a motor cutting out and men on a fishing charter swearing.

Like any band of their ilk, they knew to whom they'd been assigned. Every band that was larger than a soloist or a duo went to two people. Only two. There were no exceptions. The two people were together, and you were together with them. Now, should something happen to the two people, matters could get dicey. You had a few options, but it's not like you became a free agent, so to speak. It was considered bad form to even think about trying to shoehorn other musicians out of their established gigs, and as for bartering and trading places: pairing people— as a duo—with a new ensemble just like that, was asking for formlessness and despair. And with formlessness. and despair, there'd be a lot of bands without their proper gigs, and there were only so many motors in the world for a fellow to pick up part-time work on, and only so many mackerel, presumably, that you could hoodwink with an ace harmonica player.

They got their initial booking in March. This was not the most typical month. The summer season was more common. The people who were together in March tended to have been together before that. There were statistical studies done by some members of the band's union. But one took work—and you were only getting that single chance—where you could get it. The couple seemed nice enough. Nice couples, though, meant standard sets. You could never get too "out there," as some of the more experienced bands put it, when everything was mild and docile and peaceful.

To offset this, and alleviate your boredom as a musician, and the most subtle kind at that, certain promises were made: like the right to pick out a copse of one's choosing, after both members of the couple had departed the earth, to live out one's day, making the music that marked a given copse—in sound, anyway—as different from any other. So even if you had to adhere to a familiar set list as you soundtracked the latest romantic evening—and how beneath him HP thought it was to play notes suggestive of crackling hearth fires or people applauding at a wedding, or the sounds that came with flesh entering flesh—you would have your opportunity for individuality, eventually.

There was little set list variation for the first six months. Still, the hours weren't long, and with the bump in pay from finally landing a regular gig, the members of the band were able to indulge themselves. There was no more need to reside in gutters, drains, or the crooks of trees, as in the lean years. BE took up residence in a sprawling, abandoned beehive, where raucous parties were held, which had the effect of producing a loud buzzing sound, so loud that duos—couples, that is—out on long nature walks with their own bands in tow kept a wide berth, and the saturnalia raged on.

It wasn't until half a year passed that the band was able to let rip and get creative. There were glasses that their woman wore. They knew her as Mounts, because they never could get quite close enough, with their size and all, to hear her name properly, and Mounts seemed pretty close, near as they could tell, plus she was awfully tall. The man they knew as Tuck. BE had attempted to remark that the man liked to talk tough, but no one could ever understand what BE said, especially after all of the parties back at the hive, which seemed to have done something to his mouth. So Tuck it was.

They rocked out behind him in the rain in the town where Mounts lived. The door was locked, and Tuck was going anywhere but inside, it seemed. As his anguish deepened, Stafford commanded his band mates—with a vigorous series of waves—to play harder, and so the rain came down louder, and Tuck's hair began to look like it was dripping into his face. Eventually, Mounts appeared, Tuck went inside, and the band picked up their instruments and proceeded to try and gauge the mood as they played on the stairs, where Mounts and Tuck were sitting, the latter gesturing dramatically as Stafford gave the cue to P Squared to play a riff like the sound of baseboard heaters groaning, a flare of unease, but a lazy, idle unease, probably not an unease to be overly concerned about.

"That was some fucking gig," HP declared afterward as they rode atop the empty soda can that doubled as the tour bus. "Finally. We got to cut loose a bit."

This kind of attitude concerned Stafford. Sure, he enjoyed a musical challenge as much as anyone—and you want your band to stay tight, which requires the occasional challenge—but you didn't want to have to go all out every night, as a performing unit, to say nothing of having to give multiple gigs in a single day.

There were assorted tales of groups who became burnt out, players who lost their chops because they never got any down time and it was one intense concert after another with few or no breaks in between, so that life became one long, ever-extending gig.

When that happened, your options were limited. You could quit the racket, but what, really, were you going to do? You could team up with the dust and be someone who blankets a portion of something, or you could get work, probably, as a rubbish router, standing on the ends of

streets, telling a given napkin to go east or west or order-
ing a ketchup packet, stuck to the bottom of a car tire, to
come down from the rubber and spend some time on the
asphalt, which was more natural and would allow a child
to come along and put his or her foot atop the packet, as
this, in large part, was what packets were for, after they
had been mostly used up and cast outside. Not especially
rewarding work.

Matters, on the duo front, were peaceable for a while
after that night on the stairs. The band held a meeting to
come up with their first official name. HP, being something of a rebel, suggested the Gleaming Blades, but no
one else thought it wise to have a name so at odds with
their prevailing musical style.

"Whatever. It's bound to get intense again," he argued.
"Don't you think?"

Stafford wasn't sure. He hoped not. It had long been
a dream of his to retire to a copse of his own, preferably
one by the sea, as he found that salt air helped his sound,
and he was certain that in a remote, coastal copse with
a high saline content he'd be able to make music that
someone happening through, with the proper equip-
ment, might feel fit to record, and he'd have a record of
his own after a fashion. Who else had he ever known
who could say as much?

"I think we'll go with the Makewells for now," he over-
ruled.

"The Makewells? Are you fucking shitting me?"

P Squared laughed. You could usually count on him
encouraging HP, along with Doc, who loved nothing
more than rascally behavior, while BE simply sat and was.

When their duo was finally married, after a year of peaceable gigs for the most part, Stafford figured he was well on his way to that copse. The band harmonized with some confetti at the ceremony, and the latter was pleased to have its sound bolstered, as normally confetti could not be heard particularly well.

But a week later everything changed. They all took to the road, to the home of Tuck's parents. None of the Makewells had ever been so far from home. But it was in that new place where their longstanding name was retired and they rechristened themselves the Char Paper Blues Band, as Stafford always believed that your name could not be at odds with your sound. The latter was fiery, every night and through large chunks of the day, and instantly hot, as though they were the musical equivalent of a match brought to char paper. HP blew one molten lick after another as they all watched what Tuck did. He broke a pair of Mounts' eyeglasses on the first night, and BE was roused to activity for once when he had to dive out of the way of the falling glass, and was luckily hit only by a tear instead.

They covered up the sounds as best they could. In the basement, as Tuck was once again starting to yell, HP, ever-versatile, uncorked a solo akin to a washing machine making more noise than normal, while P Squared comped beneath him and Stafford implored the band on, despairing that he'd never get his copse.

Back home, in their normal portion of the country, they were summoned again and again to the home that Mounts and Tuck now shared together. How each of them came to dread the feeling of a hand on the shoulder, and that voice—"Come on, get up. We have to go. The soda can is waiting. We're going on again."

On and on they went. In the bathroom at the house of someone else's duo—and this was a most embarrassing thing for a band to have to endure with another so close by—at a birthday party, a scavenger hunt in the city, a swank restaurant, a Greyhound bus, the front seat of a car, the back seat of a car, several elevators, a tub, a kitchen table, a pier watching Santa Claus float into the town on the back of a lobster boat at the next Christmastime.

"This isn't working for me," HP announced as Santa chuckled and waved.

"What do you mean this isn't working for you?" demanded Stafford as he raced around the band, helping P Squared with his piano parts and standing in for an exhausted BE as they jammed, frantically, with some chiming bells and carolers, thus making something more musical of their duo's latest heated exchange. "You're playing brilliantly, mate, really. No one has ever played like you're playing. You must know that, right?"

"Of course I know it. But this isn't what I want. This sucks."

"It could change back. Of course it could. And then we'll all be blessed for having seen both sides of the ledger, and no one will complain if we end up as the Makewells again and play out the rest of our career nice and easy so we all get our copses, and we'll all keep in touch through various pieces of litter thanks to the ease of the postal system. What do you say, lads? Why, if Tuck would simply do away with the yelling—it's becoming easier, as we've all agreed, to make out what he's saying, despite our small stature—and the breaking of Mounts' assorted posses-sions, we'd be on our way back to the good old days. And better days. Hear, hear."

HP shook his head and blew the loudest, longest solo of his career to date, which had the effect of inspiring BE to flail away at his bass harder than ever before as the Christmas bells did a double-take in the center of town, trying to determine what manner of band had tripled the effect of their sound.

In the morning, Stafford got up to rouse his band-mates. They had another gig. By then, they were all living in their duo's mailbox, given the frequency with which they had to perform. There was no sense having a lengthy commute. They were all ready to go when BE shrugged his shoulders, an indication that, for the first time, HP was not standing amongst them.

"Maybe he's inside already," Stafford said to no one in particular.

He was not, but there was a note from him, on a tiny corner of Kleenex—which is to say, for them, a huge piece of letter board—outside the master bedroom door that read, "You don't get it. Good luck with the band. Yours, HP (Harmonica Player)."

An argument had just gotten underway on the other side of the door.

Stafford thought about making a joke about how the show has to go on, but instead he simply walked under the door, hoping the others would follow—which they did—and commence the latest concert, which sounded a lot like a showerhead emitting more water than ever, and skin slapping against skin for about five minutes. Most of the arguments were not resolved in this manner, but at least it took less time, and the band repaired back to the mailbox to get some sleep.

That was the pattern—minus the flesh-on-flesh parts—for the remainder of the band's time with their duo. When it was clear that a split was inevitable, the Char Paper Blues Band began to play slower. Not with less urgency, but with less freneticism, one might say. They had some choices to make: to give up the musical life, or to remain loyal to one—but not both—of the members of their crumbling duo. Perhaps not surprisingly, they opted for Mounts, and eventually matters went well enough with her—after two more Tucks—that they were able to bill themselves, at last, as the Makewells, playing to an advanced age.

When it came time for Stafford to take up residency in what he figured was his very own copse, and a copse by the water at that, where he could make a unique strain of music, hoping it would someday end up on a real record, he heard a sound somewhat reminiscent of one from a long time ago, but a sound that felt new as well, like it'd just been invented seconds before he happened along.

"What's up, Stafford?" HP began, emerging from behind a blade of grass.

"What the—"

"Relax. No point arguing about it. There are all kinds of ways to have need for the kind of band we were. At our most technically accomplished. Yelling so loud that we can almost make out what is being said is just one of them. Did you really never ask yourself what else might have been going on?"

Stafford felt ashamed. He always knew. But how he wanted that copse all for himself, even though one of their ilk had never come by a private copse through pretending they didn't know what kind of audience they were playing for.

"Side Tucks?"

"Side Tucks. So now we go halfsies. That's what happens when a band doesn't stay together for the right reasons."

This did not displease Stafford entirely. He always knew, underneath everything, that HP was the caring sort, and now that they were united in this way they might inspire others to make their own music. Who knew how these matters really worked?

"Do you think we have a band that plays for us, somewhere nearby?" Stafford asked, starting to feel himself perk up.

"Probably. So let's not be dicks to each other, all right?"

"All right."

The both listened as the sound of the waves in the not-so-far-off distance became quieter, leaving only the low chirp of the crickets of the copse, who were exactly as loud as they usually were.

THE ANGLERFISH COMEDY TROUPE

Doss WOULD HAVE PREFERRED a robe instead, but the towel, discomfiting though it was, was at least of a generous size, and after he had stapled it together at the front of his body there was a feeling, at least, of being in some form of clothes.

Every day he passed the bedroom window of the house whose locks he could not figure out. There was a complex system in place, it seemed, which no key could solve, although he had fashioned many. Or maybe it was all because of the mists, as he had once called them. The locals would have opted for fog, but he had been a more romantic sort, and his wife was prone to reading those medieval mysteries where mists play a large part as knights amble through groves with their clunky swords, cutting away brambles in search of a maiden shackled away in a cave by some snake, never mind that administering to the shackles was probably a great difficulty if you were a snake. "He must have had an unbilled assistant," Doss would comment when his wife broached the subject.

He'd watch her sleep through the fog, in her room, on the ground floor, as everyone else slept save the men who made the foghorns bellow on the harbor. There was a chance, he figured, that an audio system was in place, maybe way up in the headlands, and the foghorns were simply set on a loop, and perhaps no one else was ever outside, or not when he was, anyway.

His wife was more form than figure at that point, something under the bed sheets, but her hips rose where they ought to have risen if she were on her side, and there was what could have been the shape of her right shoulder, and her head, too, about the size of a rock that would have been heavy to lift but not too heavy to throw, although one would not have been able to throw it very far.

He knew better than to tap the glass. The moment he did so, it was back to the open plaza at what he decided was the center of the town, even though it was incongruous with all of the other parts and the town's prevailing themes of anchored boats, empty fish shacks, closed ice cream shops, and rusty metal historical markers extolling how one native had stabbed a bear in the throat upon such and such a spot and another had later shot the bear-stabber in a duel not more than fifty yards away.

"Must have been one busy strip of beach," Doss thought. "I wonder if his mind flashed back to the whole bear incident, as it was going down."

He'd want to know what his wife thought on the subject, or what her form had to say anyway, and the temptation to tap the glass, to rouse her from her bed, was sometimes too great.

But the moment he heard the blurry sound his finger made, like a piano note beneath a layer of foam, and the slurry smudge that came after it, he was back in the plaza, where he never liked to be. For there were no people here either, but angle upon angle, between the buildings, where you knew there were eyes hovering in the air. You couldn't see them properly, but if you had exceptional peripheral vision, as Doss unfortunately had, you could make them out in the most extreme corners of those peripheries.

The eyes had something to do with Doss looking so hard for a stapler, something to make his towel more formal and to stop anyone from asking if he was in search of the public baths. His sense was there were no such things in the town, and he hated to be the butt of a joke.

He'd curse himself for tapping on the glass at his fog-shrouded house, and for taking matters further and thinking that smearing his finger around on it would rouse his wife, just as he had reached below her waist and smeared his finger around, more vaguely, trying to smile as he did so. He tried to manufacture the same smile when she became unreachable and the fog first visited him.

They were friendly right from the start, he and the fog. He was surprised what the latter toted around inside itself, stuff that most people were never aware of. Consider, for instance, the light at the center of a cloud of fog that gives it a creepy glow. Turns out that's an anglerfish, with only one in place for every cubic mile of fog. It was a great honor to be selected for the post, and while the training program was not rigorous, who else, really, could the fog have asked? A monkfish?

That was one of the jokes they shared. He never saw his resident anglerfish, but Doss made frequent requests to the fog to meet him one of these days. The fog was a bit of a prick tease, admittedly, and would encourage Doss to step deeper inside, which had a vaguely sexual connotation, but that was how fog worked. Doss would go as far inside as he could without ever encountering the anglerfish—though one time he thought he saw some of its needle-like teeth at the edge of his vision, but by then he'd be in his friend's living room, outstaying his welcome.

There were more kids, it seemed, with each beer Doss drank. His friend's wife navigated her way around the kitchen, cooking something in a vast pot. Maybe they were neighbor children. Doss's friend never volunteered any information on the subject, just nodded as Doss discussed his wife in the most absolute terms he could manage.

"I don't know," he'd warble. "I don't know, I don't know. Do you know?" He knew he was embarrassing himself, and Doss's friend and Doss's friend's wife would exchange looks that they thought he couldn't see, but again, few people had Doss's type of peripheral vision.

"I mean, it's not like I hit her or cheated on her. Kicked her down the stairs." He'd work himself up, like he was Jimmy Stewart in that movie where he works in politics and filibusters, but then one of the new kids—and it was always one of the new ones—would tug at his pant leg and ask, "What did you do then?"

Sometimes the fog would roll back in and save him with a quiet getaway. The fog was considerate enough that once he got back inside, there'd be a waiting cup of what he figured the fog thought of as coffee. It was more like coffee-flavored water, and quite disgusting, but he was glad to have it anyway, and glad for the friendship.

Back at the window, he'd marvel at how his wife, or what he assumed was his wife, never changed positions. Her head never got above the blankets, and given that knocking on the glass or smearing his finger across it was not working, he took to throwing stones.

This was more enjoyable, enough so that the fog got involved as well and eventually mastered the art of flicking pebbles in a more or less straight line. When the fog announced that the anglerfish—a most keen thinker, given how much time he was able to devote to rumination on the bottom of the sea, where not much went on—had advised trying to break the glass with a rock about the size of his wife's head, Doss was perplexed.

"I thought you said that the anglerfish was an unrivaled wiseass, a veritable master of abyssal plain comedy?"

The fog did not recall being so articulate, but it was pleasing that Doss thought of him in such regard. And, truth be told, the anglerfish was a wiseass. But then again, that was the nature of most everyone on the abyssal plain, which was where the fog, contrary to what most people knew, originated. It was also where the fog enjoyed spending the bulk of its time, serving as set dressing for everyone it had ever brought there, so that they could enact their part in the modes of drama that were so specific to the place, with their mixture of comedy and...what was that word the people used?

"Pain," Doss broke in. "Pain, fog."

The fog, as was its way, would lessen over time and drift away, and Doss would be left to himself, in the towel that he had fashioned into a form of clothing as best he could, to stare at his wife's form as night came on, and the moon cursed out the fog in the manner of one who hates to be obscured. The fog then returned to where it had originated to watch another drama unfold, the anglerfish providing a rough-hewn form of direction, having once read the preface to a book about medieval theatre.

In the clear night, even with the moon egging him on, Doss was unable to lift the rock that was roughly the size of his wife's head. Ingress simply did not seem possible. For some reason—perhaps it was his desperation—he tried blowing on the glass. Like that would do anything. As he did so, he heard a voice that may or may not have been his wife's. He wasn't able to tell, for sure, as the fog emerged, to the moon's horror, from inside the glass, fanning outward and making off with Doss for the latest night of abyssal plain theatre. "I'm not in here," the voice said. "I never was. Not like you thought. Now...go."

"Go where?" Doss asked no one in particular.

"How should I know?" came the answer, from the corner of his eye, where some needle-like objects glinted in the bright lights of the stage. "Now, are we going to enact this, or are we going to enact this? Fog! Dim the lights, if you please."

The fog was too respectful to point out to the anglerfish that any and all lights were a result of his personage, and no one else's, with even the moon having begged off for the night.

DIBS ON BLOOD

HE THOUGHT, AT FIRST, that a string had come loose from his sock. There had not been a lot of shopping since she'd left. So when he sat down in his chair in the corner of his room, where he had mounted a small mirror, a coaster, and a small fan into the wall—a straight-edged razor balanced, best he could manage, on the coaster—he was annoyed at first, and then curious, but not curious enough to stand up and try to get a view of whatever it was that was scratching at the lower portion of his calf.

He was pleased with the results of his carpentry. It had taken some doing to get the coaster into the wall, as it was made of sandstone and kept crumbling to bits in his hands as he worked the drill. But eventually some epoxy saw him through, and he determined that she would have been pleased.

Décor was always his department, as he liked to say, but the actual execution of hanging a wedding photo or a movie poster on any of the walls of the house they shared was beyond him. Still, he was adroit at standing and pointing, uttering, "A little more to the left, up now... just a bit, perfect. No. Actually, that's wrong. You did it wrong. More to the right."

Now that he was making do for both of them, he felt added pressure as he constructed the centerpiece of his room—which is to say, its southernmost corner, where his chair was. The chair had wheels, and it wouldn't allow him to get as close to the wall as he had hoped, for every time his head bounced off of it, he'd roll back to the center of the room, the last place he wanted to be.

"The center is a bit tricky," he thought many times in those new digs.

The hole was pretty consistent in its behavior. It wasn't like those holes he had read about, at night when he was asleep, dreaming he was reading. It had been different when he was a boy—back then, he'd stay up all night, reading until the morning. But that wasn't possible. Or was it? Boys have to sleep. He wasn't sure, though, that he hadn't somehow managed to go years without it. Someone would have noticed. His mother, probably. A mother would have to. Unless—well, unless something unprecedented and nontraditional was going on, something beyond a mother's view, to say nothing of a boy's.

But he had his dead father for that. His father would have noticed if he never slept, although it might have been a real challenge getting word to anyone. That seemed like a cruel lot: having to notice something about a loved one that no one else could, something of real importance, but without a voice to speak up about your vital discovery.

Or maybe it wasn't so vital. After all, here he was, all these years later, in his corner, where he had, at last, managed to mount his small mirror, sandstone coaster, fan, and straight-edged razor. It was a bravura performance as far as he was concerned. And taking the wheels off of the chair—that just added to the achievement. It was in the corner that he decided he must have been first reading, and then dreaming he was reading, and that his father hadn't spoken up because there was no real danger, so there was no real danger in reading now, while he slept, and that is how he learned that some rooms have holes that grow and grow and grow until the room is no more, although the surrounding rooms—if they belong to someone else—are free to carry on as they were.

That seemed equitable to him. It wasn't like his hole should be his neighbor's burden, or vice versa, though he assumed—with a decent amount of conviction—that his neighbor did not have a hole like his. And while this was fascinating—he didn't see how you could think otherwise—it was troubling, too.

There weren't a lot of people to whom you could express your concerns. There had been his wife, with her skills in hanging things. It wasn't long after the hole got out of his thoughts—where it had started, and where he had manfully managed to contain it—and taken up residence in the northernmost corner of the bedroom of their house that he began to deliberate whether it was right to send her down into it. To recon, so to speak. With a rope around her waist. He wasn't going to just chuck her in.

But he could never state his aims directly. He tried to cajole her as if by some secret code, for which he hoped she had a key somewhere inside of her, as he had once had his hole inside of him. Some things you just didn't say aloud. He didn't know why; it just felt that way. The surety was overwhelming. So he cajoled more and more, and contorted his face as if those contortions were their own varieties of skeleton keys. He'd jump up and down in the middle of the room.

"I'm not exercising, you know," he'd shout, as his head came ever nearer to the ceiling, until he had tired himself out. The floor was so sturdy there, in the center of that room. Then he would turn to the northernmost corner and shudder as best as he could, so that his body trembled and became liquidish, like a vibrating column of water.

But if his wife saw the hole, she said nothing. This angered him. Maybe she was in cahoots with the hole. They were double-teaming him. But maybe the hole counted for more than one entity. Who knew how well it hid its numbers. It was a hole. So they could have been quadruple-teaming him. He trembled again at the mathematical possibilities.

Worse was when he thought he saw the top of his father's head coming out of the hole. Or going back down into it. Right by the baseboards. Then again, he hadn't seen his father's head in an exceedingly long time. Still, this wasn't the easiest thing to have to witness, even though he wasn't sure exactly what he was witnessing.

Perhaps the head belonged to someone else entirely. He got his favorite chair—with wheels—and put it in the center of the room. And there he sat, watching. While his wife was somewhere else. He watched for as long as his eyes could take it, until he began to believe that he could feel the blood traveling between them. First the left had more blood, then the right. Or the right would hog the blood and the left would grow much wearier, so that he'd shake his head violently, or else slap himself in the face, to get the right eye to share with its compatriot.

He remembered how he and his wife played dibs. She had played it as a little girl. You had to call dibs if you wanted something and there was just one thing to want. A last piece of cake. The final drops of Merlot at the southernmost portion of the bottle. The passenger seat, if there was someone else with you. But there rarely was. It was just the two of them. He wondered if his eyes were playing a similar game with their blood, which was, to be technical, his blood, although he suspected they viewed the matter differently.

Infrequently, he heard his wife's voice behind him as he sat in his chair, duty bound, watching the hole in the northernmost corner of their bedroom. *Come away, come away*, it seemed to say, although he could never tell, definitively, given his extreme focus with his more pressing business.

But when the voice dissipated—if it had ever really been there at all—he noticed that the hole would expand, like it was making for him, in the center of the room where he had figured a hole could never go.

The next time he thought he heard his wife's voice, with its vague incantation—*come away, come away*—he raised his right hand as quick and sharply as possible, like he thought a military dictator would. The voice stopped. He did not have to worry about hearing it again, at least. There was a fluttering of footsteps, and the sound of someone—wearing layer upon layer of socks—jumping up and down violently, as he once had, in the center of that very room where his chair now was. He thought he heard a vague fluttering sound at the bottom of the hole, although, to be practical in the matter, he had been sitting in his chair for a remarkably long time.

That particular voice did not trouble him again, but as the hole stopped growing, he discovered that he had little reason to remain in the house. The phenomenon had been so singular that he remained in his chair for an indeterminate amount of time—time was no longer the same, anyway—but, eventually, the house and the voice shifted into memories that he tried to stuff down into another hole that had taken up residence in his mind. Holes, he figured, were useful when used properly. You could sequester a lot of unpleasant things in a hole.

But his latest hole was not as practical as he had hoped it would be. She kept popping out of it. Not literally, as his father, perhaps, had. And while he was sure her voice would not register on a tape recorder with its refrain of *come away, come away,* he heard it in his head nonetheless, which was a kind of hearing, he supposed, and it was that kind of hearing he blamed for helping the hole get out of his head and into the center of his room.

It was a different room now. A faraway room. A room that, were it introduced to the initial room, would not have much to say. He decided that if he were a room—he tried to be empathetic—that would be crucial to lighten the mood and diffuse the awkwardness of the introduction.

The hole spread and spread and spread until it got to the edge of what one might consider the outer fringes of the middle of the room. He had a decent idea that it'd stop there, because a hole would probably want to leave a little extra space for itself, so that it could be observed. He'd been through this before, and while not an expert in holes by any means, he was certain he knew more than most people. He tried to make the best of the situation, which meant finding a new way to observe this latest hole, to keep everything fresh. At the same time, this seemed as fine an opportunity as any to work at becoming handy.

The mirror was not hard to mount. He had some glue. His wife would have found a more traditional means of mounting it, but the result, more or less, was the same. The sandstone coaster was all he had from the first room, the room that would not have anything to say to this present one. He wondered if maybe a common object would somehow bind the two, such that if he ever had reason to try and find his wife, they could repair to their old home, and maybe take some of the finer pieces from his new one without offending anyone.

Like his straight razor, and his fan. The razor fell a lot, and sometimes it sliced through one of his feet, or even bounced off one foot to slice the other. He noticed in the mirror that the hole would appear to undulate somewhat when this happened, but undulating was not the same as growing. No one could deny that. Not even his eyes, which would grow weary, both of them, each time some blood came out of his feet or legs, but he knew they were faking, and were simply gluttons for the stuff.

He was ashamed of them. After all this time, after all this solid observing, in two rooms now with holes, this was how they conducted themselves. He made with the razor like he was going to cut into one of them. They couldn't help but see it in the mirror, just as the hole got a view. But he simply scraped the blade against his face with a scoring motion, flicking out a little blood. "I'll waste it if you're not careful. Don't make me waste it. We have enough to tend to here."

The mini fan blew the blood dry, and he didn't have to suffer the uncomfortable feeling of having wet cheeks, nor seeing wet cheeks, in the mirror, as he had so often with his wife, although those were not his cheeks. At the time, that did not make it worse, but now it did. He had to be careful when he got to thinking like this, because the hole, being a hole, was ever-opportunistic, and if it got confident enough it might make a lunge for him, and he hadn't any rope, nor anything to tie himself to, that would ensure he'd come out again.

Still, he hadn't counted on that feeling that first came from what he thought was a loose bit of thread from one of his socks. The sensation was like being touched by a moth in the shape of a ribbon. A fluttering. But when he finally tore his gaze away from the mirror, after the latest shenanigans of the eyes and the undulating hole, he saw that he wasn't wearing any socks. There was another hole, he discovered, only this time it was the size of a puncture mark, the sort that one would make with the dull prong of an unwound paper clip. A white fiber was growing out of this tiniest of holes in the back of his leg, at the bottom of his calf. He pulled it, but it did not come out.

Later, after some indiscriminate amount of time had passed, he saw a second white thread, and then another, and then so many he could not count them. He took his razor to the hole and cut it out, making a larger hole, as the hole in the center of his room seemed to undulate and progress at once, but it was hard to tell, with so much going on.

The tingling, fluttering feeling spread. He cut so many holes out of himself that he was relieved the white strands remained behind to cover everything up. He kept cutting—even the eyes couldn't bear to look, after a certain point, despite their previous gluttony—just as he kept hearing that voice in his head, which he began to think would now register on a tape recorder if he had one.

On the day he realized that he was now a hole himself, for so much had been cut away, and looked forward to having some common ground, or lack thereof, with the hole in the center of his room, he noted sadly that it was no longer there.

"Ah," he thought as the fan blew against what had been his cheeks. "So that's how they work."

DUENDE RULES

Does anything give more away than a contrast? The way you came to me then, the way you come to me now. I turn from where I sit and start with the bed. It's like a movie theater, isn't it? What will play tonight? What will I see? And so interactive. Like a choose-your-own-adventure book, but without the free will. Still, there I am in it every night. One would think there'd be a respite. But no. Maybe I'm an entertainer. Maybe there are people, or entities, off somewhere watching me in my latest movie. Last night: some country town. There was a sheriff, crafty sheriff. The kind you knew was against you but stayed friendly toward you as he built his case. Like that police guy in *Crime and Punishment*. Someone who gets in your head. You had yet to make an appearance at this point. There were two forests. Massive forests. Between them, flat land, sans trees, like a grassy, yellowed road that stretched and stretched, keeping one forest from the other. A high school classmate was with me. A troublemaker. But a harmless one. More an annoyance to teachers than anything. Had to write an essay about henchman and villainous assistants one time. He asked the teacher how to spell Azrael, that cat from *The Smurfs*. Everyone called him Boner. Every high school probably has a kid named Boner. But now he was Bones. Focused, steady of purpose. A partner of mine, for some reason, but in what capacity I wasn't aware of. I was out doing errands for you. They were fairly nautical in theme. The procuring of some sea salt, some chum. We were going chumming, for what, I don't know. There were never any fishing rods in the house, there was no boat, and you had left me anyway. But I wanted to get up early and do something regarding us, put in a full day if I could. Kept seeing that sheriff, though, and Bones making plans of his own, racing across the town, he and I meeting up a lot near that grassy road between the two giant forests.

They've gotten longer. There used to be just one scene a night, or, when the story deserved it, an installment several nights in a row, like the movie theater. This bed you have probably forgotten—and it was just an ordinary bed back then, with sheets you disapproved of—had decided to feature serials. But last night, when dusk came on and I was still at the edge of that grassy road, wondering what errand I might be able to do for us, thinking maybe a large conch shell would prove useful in being able to talk with you again, as though conch shells were useful for bartering in these matters, or, that failing, could be used as instruments one might talk into, to reach a person across an otherwise unspannable gap, I knew this would be a full feature.

The rain had started when Bones came out from behind a rock, pinched my elbow, and said, "Now." I understood what he meant. We put a lot of distance between us and the start of that grassy road that evening. But that was the thing about the grassy road: flanked as it was by violent-looking forests, so dark that Hansel and Gretel would have found their wandering ways reformed before they'd ever been able to indulge themselves, you could see across miles and miles of it, like it was inside a telescope that you looked through from the end you happened to be on.

I knew a lot of this had to do with the sheriff. Still, I didn't expect to see him advance, from miles back—it was hard to gauge the distance, you understand—in the morning after keeping up that pace all night long. Why hadn't we taken to the woods? You wouldn't have needed to go as far to free yourself from a pursuer, I believed, given how muddled everything was bound to get in there. And caves. You could find a cave and go into it. But once you were in a cave, you were all in, totally dependent upon the quality of your hiding spot. This led to a cutaway in which I found myself, sans Bones, under a house I used to live in long before I knew you. I'd told you about it, how a puppy-love girlfriend and I snuck up into this crawlspace that no one ever went into, and where, the thinking went, no one would look for you, although, if they did, it was game over. We never had crawlspaces, you and I. Maybe you did. Maybe they were out in the open, but I couldn't see them, or you in them, but there you were, in your own cave every day. I never came in, so you snuck out the back door, which your cave, unlike most, happened to have. But now we took to the forest, the one on the left. It was like a forest of Christmas trees without any of the festive trappings. One slid into those woods down a ramp, not unlike how you had slid down that little hill on the last Christmas we spent together, going to the pond to see if the beaver and his missus had any yuletide plans of their own. Things were getting dicey by now, and I gave Bones a look as if to say, "How can anyone be gaining on us? Why are the dogs getting louder?" I had a cracked cell phone in my pocket. The only kind of cell phone that would even pull up your number, and the reason why I always kept a small hammer with me, in case I had need of breaking a phone to try and reach you. Not that I ever thought, by any miracle, you'd pick up. But it was a reoccurring plot point of these films. Maybe the producers were simply trying to give the viewers—whoever they were—what they had come to expect and enjoy.

Leave it to Bones to have a plan. He walked with purpose, which is why I followed him as resolutely as I did. Another rock, this time, bigger than the one from which he'd emerged. A bag behind. And in the bag, two people—a man and a woman, not young, not old, probably older than they looked, clearly in love. "Now we have leverage," Bones announced, as a flash of anger came across the young man's face, and the woman with him cast her eyes down and looked sad, defeated. Aware that fight or flight would do no good. There was talk from the young man that the forest was populated by goblins and the like; he called them *duendes*, believing a learned attitude would help sell his story, but all we encountered was a train. Stopped, seemingly unattended, and clumped with moss and brambles, but which became filled with light—albeit gaslight—the moment we climbed aboard. Bones threw some tickets over his shoulder to join the pine needles on the forest floor below. Finally, a way to outpace that sheriff who was smarter than you would have thought, with his ability to be all friendly and gain your trust as he was breaking you down, and your motives, in his mind, building his case. Bones was not a heartless individual, and he was kind enough to bestow a slice of pizza on each of our companions, the woman swapping hers for the man's as it had more cheese on top, and this, apparently, was what he preferred, just as she preferred for him to be the happier member of the couple. It was quite touching actually, even if the man did not thank her, but then again, they probably were both quite ravenous—he especially, if he had done more of the work during their time in the forest. But who was to know how they divvied all of that up. And who was to know that the sheriff had boarded this same train and was advancing from coach to coach. I thought about trying you on the cracked cell phone, as this certainly qualified as one of those moments, in times past, when I would have needed your counsel, and you would have been the first person I turned to, desperate for the safety you always provided me. But it was time for flight, and I worried that if I lost the cracked cell phone in all of that commotion I would not be able to get another. The young man was apparently an able thought reader, and he advised that there were *duendes*—these goblin fellows of his—that would cut me a good deal on a cracked cell phone that was sure to get you on the line and commence a period of communication that would lead to a future, but I knew how impossible that was, and I resolved to keep my guard up against him.

We were fortunate that our coach stopped while all of the others kept advancing, and the sheriff, and his men and his dogs, overshot us. But if I knew that sheriff, I knew we'd be seeing him again. Still, it was nice to have some time to rest. We could afford just the one hotel room for all four of us, but it was a sprawling, L-shaped room. Bones was at the top of the L in a large bed. I was down at the ninety-degree angle. The couple were on my right, at the far edge of the letter, in a sleeping bag from which their heads never emerged, although I could hear first laughter, then whispers, then arguing whispers, crying, and a harsh kind of laughter from the man. I could not sleep. I remembered someone once telling me that cracked cell phones were more likely to produce the desired effect were they used in concert with a television that broadcast the same image over and over again, and since I had some time and the television showing nothing more than a shot of the room, I walked over to it and tried you, again. I had long arrived at the point when hearing your voice on your message destroyed me from the inside out all over again and caused me to miss you more, love you more, detest you more, and wonder anew how that creature possessing that voice could have wanted this for us. I think it might have been easier if the message had changed, if it was different from before you left—but it was not, and so I struggled with being in that room, with those three people, and feeling like I was somewhere else at the same time, a place where I could procure the stuff one procures on errands—more common/useful goods, in all probability, than chum— and bring it all back to you.

We did not make it until morning. Bones had been de-
liberating in his portion of the L. The couple would be
confronted. "Did you actually do the killing?" he asked
the man, as everyone gathered around the sleeping bag.
"Because it looks like you did. Given that we have this
here." He produced a cloth bag and dumped out the head
of another man. "Is this not the man she once loved?"
Bones asked. They agreed that it was. "But it's not like you
think," the man continued. "Oh," said Bones. "What is
it, then?" The woman looked away, toward the television
set, where I had been trying to reach you. "We found him
dead," the man said. "And it seemed wise to try and send a
message. To sever the past, if you will. So we—I—cut off
his head. Surely there's no crime in that. Or not a serious
one, anyway." I watched Bones chew this over for a while
in the darkness, as I did the same. Finally, he said, "No,
it would not be an outrageous crime, if he were already
dead. But it is the order of things that we must establish. It
would be more useful, of course, to you, if he were already
dead, but that would not be ideal for us. We will have to
go to court before trying to do anything with that sheriff." This seemed reasonable.

In the morning we left for a house I used to live in,
which had been greatly modified. I knew you would be
there. That's why I did not call. One reason. The man,
whose spirit appeared to be quashed, advised me that too
many calls in too short a time could lead to some *duende*
issuing an order that would prevent me from ever being
able to stop thinking about you. And how I longed to be
able to forget, going so far as to barter with a hecate which
a friend—a former book club companion—had introduced

me to, offering first my sight, then my hearing, then half of my intellect, and, finally, as all hecates prefer, my soul. But it was still no dice. The hecate did not wish to assume my emotional debt.

I knew the house would have been overhauled, but I did not expect to see the bathroom sinks and toilets outside, affixed to the easternmost wall, where the shade was, thanks to those pitch pines. But this only meant there was more space in the meeting room. Everyone had a turn in what had once been the bathroom. You looked good, but very dry, like a piece of char paper. Or as though you were made of flax. You could have done a wonderful job blending in with the yellows of the grassy road where Bones first took my elbow and we began our escape. In the past, I thought of you more like a rivulet or a sluice or, the majority of the time, a saltwater river, someone who led into something bigger, a smaller form from which so much grew and so much life was fed. They would not allow us a moment alone in that meeting room, and I knew that was because you had set this up in advance, and your orders were to be respected. "Told you," the man said, as the sheriff, who finally turned up, led him away, while Bones counted his money—he earned it—on the back of the horse the sheriff had gifted him. It fell to me to find a place to dispose of the head we had been carrying around, having signed the forms that said I could not try and stuff it in one of the toilets outside, or weigh it down with ballast so that it would sink to the bottom of any rivulet, sluice, or saltwater river within an infinite number of miles. Needless to say, the hecate—and I knew but the one—would not be taking it either.

CONGER

THERE WAS A CERTAIN LIGHTNESS, an ease of life, it was commonly believed, in being able to smell better than you could see. True, one had a tendency to bump into rocks and beds of kelp and struggle, on occasion, with finding routes out of a given reef, but smells rarely posed problems, and did little in terms of inducing fear.

That was the old saw, anyway. The conger eel wasn't so sure. But perhaps that was because his own normally heightened sense of smell was diminishing. Gone were the days when he could detect a seal carcass that had floated to the bottom of the sea simply by angling himself in the current and swimming against it, letting one wonderful scent after another fire his imagination.

But with his diminished sense of smell came something that he had never expected, something which frightened him, never mind that eels of his sort were famously—in that particular community—believed to have no fear of anything, not even the dogfish who'd make the occasional lunge. And this was against a backdrop of darkness, for eels had the good fortune, as these things were commonly believed, to be nearly blind and thus oblivious to most terrors. The lobsters who lived for decades longer than anyone else regarded them as the stalwarts of the sea, for any lobster who had lived more than twenty years had, naturally, seen his share of action sequences involving everything from sperm whales and squid to men to barracuda to the various crab v. crab entanglements that tended to take place late at night, in the most forlorn back corridors of reefs rarely visited.

So it was with some shock that everyone beheld the conger eel, once so indomitable, swimming in circles. A hermit crab, being a wag, suggested that maybe the conger eel's sense of smell had gone wrong—perhaps he had crashed into the bottom of one of the boats high above, as conger eels were sometimes known to do—and was now mistaking a portion of himself for a wounded flounder, or maybe a mackerel, which had a similarly oily constitution.

The conger eel jerked through the water in violent, spastic motions, so at odds with his previously supple movements, which had been the envy of many members of that particular community, one which put a special emphasis on how adroitly you could move from place to place. There was, for instance, much talk of ripples. The leading octopus—which is to say, the sole octopus of that stretch of the ocean—being an unrivaled thinker, had attempted to quantify this fascination with ripples through a series of metrics, but while he advised the need to examine this so-called ripple quotient in relation to other members of the community, the crabs, lobsters, barracuda, mackerels, even the scallops tuned him out, and instead cited the brilliance of the conger eel and how he managed to pass through the water like the light from above: that is, without rippling it at all.

That, of course, was before he started to see. He tried to dim his eyes at first, hoping that would make his sense of smell return, and his accustomed blindness with it, but no luck. He found that he couldn't so much as go three meters—three measly meters—without needing to pause, sending ripples in every direction, thinking he had caught sight of a squid lying in wait for him behind the calcium-quoined wall of the main reef where the jellyfish usually hung out. The main reef was supposed to be a haven. You trusted the main reef. You met your friends there. Maybe you made dinner plans there. Sometimes there'd be a feast, when one of those dead seals—or, better still, a dead dolphin—floated down from higher up.

The conger eel enjoyed a rotten dolphin carcass more than just about anything, for he had great respect for dolphins, and being something of a progressive thinker—or at least he tried to be—he viewed the consumption of rotten dolphin fat and muscle as a way to help that now-departed fellow live on, only, eel style, inside the mind, body, and soul of the district's finest swimmer.

Actually, the conger eel had never thought in terms of souls until he was cursed with the ability to see. The slightest noise that made his heart feel like it was going to pop out of him—how he hated that pounding, and how it made his gills throb—and even though he had once enjoyed vomiting, because, after all, there was the wonderful aroma of whatever one had just regurgitated, it sickened him now, because it spoke to something deeper inside of himself, something less pleasingly topical. It spoke, most of all, to just how much fear he could feel, and what that fear did to a mind that had been—even in those dark moments, when no single image ever came clear to him—highly ordered. Or focused, anyway.

But now he watched, with a clarity of vision the squid would have envied, as lampreys huddled in inky corners by kelp beds you'd think no one ever went to, the group breaking apart as he came near as though there were grave secrets that had to be protected. He swam to the surface, ripples everywhere, and observed the faces of children staring down at him, just out of reach, pointing. A hand came his way, and he gingerly took a bite, not pressing his jaws all the way down lest there was something sharp, an object that might pierce him.

Great pity was taken upon the conger eel when he could not so much as bite the soft hand of a child. The rock crab, a notorious hoarder who had strips of horse flesh from the time the great boat—great in that it had so many creatures none of them had ever laid eyes on before—sank and came their way years ago, took the time to visit the conger eel in his nook in the reef, where he had lived for so long, his head hanging out, keen to let everyone know he was at home, lest someone wanted to visit. But now he huddled at the back of that nook, trembling. The rock crab laid a couple strips of horse skin at the entranceway and sighed some bubbles when the once glorious conger eel meekly pressed his lower jaw against one, unable to will himself to bite down.

The rock crab was one who would normally feel slighted, even insulted, in a situation like this, because it was not often he shared anything with anyone, being a prideful creature. He also had an odd Messiah complex—something which was very rare on the reef—and when the conger eel refused the strips of horse, the rock crab offered his own flesh instead, believing that were the conger eel to pierce him with his needle-like teeth, the rock crab would not only be saving a soul—for the rock crab had lately been spending a good deal of time with the octopus and picking up on his progressive way of thinking—but setting himself up for the kind of glory that he figured would go along with being the one crab, above all others, that everyone discussed, and would always discuss, and their offspring, too.

Still, the conger eel refused. Those that could go to the surface would follow him there on his excursions, which were becoming more frequent, as if he wanted to leave his fears behind him at the bottom of that bay. They'd all seen this before from a barracuda, who, wishing to preserve his mouth—as was a barracuda's privilege—but not his life, had stuck himself on a hook, right at his midsection. His flesh was tough in that area, and it was said that he had to keep twisting his dorsal fin, over and over, and drive himself down on the hook, so that it wouldn't come out of his searing flesh as he was pulled up to the surface and the last drop of water fell from his gills.

This was shudder-inducing, even for the minnows, who knew nothing but fear and who regarded the rock crab as the rock crab regarded the squid. But there they all were, with the rock crab on the back of a trusted mackerel, right below the water's surface. They assumed the conger eel was certainly more terrified, more riddled with fear, than he had ever been before, with the entire community behind him, like maybe an officially sanctioned attack had been planned. Everyone, of course, had seen how jittery he became whenever he came across a few members of the community engaged in what most believed were harmless activities. Two barracudas, in fact, had been plotting against him, believing that the conger eel had something to do with the downfall of their friend, who had impaled his middle portion on the hook. There was the rumor that the conger eel, beginning to see and questioning his character, had compelled the barracuda to do the same, and the latter was overwhelmed by what he found, or did not find, there.

There was no way everyone was going to miss what they figured was about to happen with the conger eel. They all saw the hook, the glinting monstrosity of it, as it broke the surface of the water, just as they all saw the hand of the woman that hung down over the side of the boat. The conger eel swam—weirdly, without ripples—toward both, and opened his powerful jaws as far as they would go. Everyone smelled the blood before they saw it, for that is how these matters work. The rock crab alone gave a salute—a subtle wave of his claw—as the conger eel descended back toward the bottom with a finger in his mouth and a hard-won yearning for more.

PLAYING IN ROOM B

THERE WAS A TACIT UNDERSTANDING that the film memorabilia room and the movie screening room were not only different, but so much so that no one was ever to watch a movie in the portion of the house that was decked out in one-sheet posters, lobby cards, and theater art, or hang anything in the chamber—he liked to call it a chamber—where films were watched.

He thought this wise; after all, you wouldn't want to be distracted when you were watching a Hitchcock movie by, say, a framed advert with Hitchcock's face on it telling you how wonderful the movie was.

"You can think of it like two distinct ecosystems, if you'd like," he told his wife. "Sure, there are some fish—catfish, I think—who can live in both salt and fresh water, but by and large, proper divisions make for better opportunities for growth. Don't you think?"

His wife had few thoughts on the matter. The aquatic comparison was to be expected. It was not uncommon for her to come down from the bedroom in the morning in search of her husband, knowing he was probably out on the headlands, the cliffs—more like sloping hills—down the street from where they lived, overlooking the water, perhaps with his video camera, shooting footage of a man pulling up his lobster traps, or maybe the harbor master cruising around. It seemed that her husband regarded the harbor master as a key character in a drama he had mapped out in his head. She was simply pleased when he would invite her to sit beside him and watch whatever he had shot, although such invitations were coming less and less frequently.

There had been times when he paused the video and made what he felt quite certain was an astute comment: maybe about how a camera appeared to pass through the glass of a window, or how a particular shot was both an homage and an extension to something Godard had once attempted, or maybe Welles.

He liked when his wife showed enthusiasm. A few questions would do. When he was alone, he'd play a game with himself, trying to guess what she might ask: where his inspiration had come from, perhaps, or how long it had taken him to think through a given shot.

That one was his favorite, because his answer, he suspected, would always be the same, and yet exceedingly impressive.

"It just came to me," he figured he'd say, "and that's the thing about when things just come to you—you can't really time it, can you? Things in your mind happen at a rate, one might say, that things do not out in the world. Everything can get stacked on top of everything else in your mind; things don't have to get laid out sequentially, like they do outside, in life. I mean, maybe while that idea about the composition for the harbor master—when he confronted the lobsterman for trying to keep lobsters that were below legal size—was working itself out, I was thinking, at the same time, about us, and how, eventually, I'll have everything ordered. You'll be able to talk to me. Well, I guess maybe that won't ever happen. You not knowing who you are and everything. I could see there coming a day when you said something like, 'I am so lost. I don't know who I am. Do I like pizza? I don't even know. I try to please people though. I'm like a computer program. People enter code on me, and I do my best to do as they wish. You won't tell me I have no soul anymore. Or make jokes about the bird shit outside, by the front door, which I never cleaned up, and you said maybe it was the closest thing I had to a friend, and I wanted to keep it around.' So I was thinking about all of that, maybe, and whether I could get everything with myself sorted—the drinking, the yelling, not making you cry. I'd also be thinking about the feasibility of helping you, after accepting that you just weren't going to be talking much, and I was going to have to use a lot of patience, a lot of selflessness, to try and help you, even if a portion of me had to accept that all of that effort might never pay off as I'd like it to. By which I mean, fix anything. Not fully, anyway. But to love you all the same. All the more? Yes. I guess. To love you all the more. Could someone like me be up to that? I know what you'd say—you'd say yes. Would you think yes? I don't know the answer to your question, though, about how long it took me to come up with the idea for the shot—a really nice low-angle shot, looking up, with the water, some clouds, the horizon, and everything in between, all in the frame—given everything else one tends to think about, or sense, when asked any one single question."

But he knew the question would never come, just as he wouldn't be able to voice any of those fleeting thoughts that ran along—or so he imagined—the back portions of his head, near the base of his right ear, where there was a bump in his skull.

He wasn't even aware of those thoughts, really, but that's what the videos were for, because he could look at himself, as he was then, and see, in his own cinematic artwork, how different everything once was.

He had remembered her smiling a lot in those films. They never went far, being fond of the entire region, which was surrounded by the ocean.

"Imagine if I could do for the ocean what Truffaut did for Paris, or Hitchcock for San Francisco. I mean, think about it—it's the ocean. We're talking massive. Seemingly endless."

So they'd go to various outcrops of rock on the shore, in their town, in neighboring towns, and he'd hold the camera up to his wife, thinking how beautiful her smile was, plus a range of other ideas, impressions, queries, and answers, as was the nature of trying to think any one single thing.

There were what he thought of as "drier" scenes, too, for contrast. Like at the farm they went to, open to the public, where goats wandered around, geese, strange ducks that weren't mallards, mallards.

In the spring, there were pigs. Two—piglets. He watched as she smiled—there it was again (or was it putting in its first appearance? He'd have to look at the film rushes, to be sure)—when the pigs played together, cautioning, "I hope you don't get too attached to them. This is a farm, after all. This spring's pigs won't be next spring's pigs, if you get my meaning."

She smiled all the same, but sadly, not unlike—the rushes confirmed—she smiled at him.

He got one of his better action sequences at that farm, one day in the winter, when the place was closed to the public. They were there so often that the owners recognized them on sight and even invited them to play hockey on the frozen pond that abutted the rabbit hutches.

There were no animals out in winter. "Why don't you check in the barn?" he suggested, staying back himself, his camera ready for the shot when his wife was chased back outside again. "I guess it's like a club in there, during the winter," he said. They joked about that action sequence a lot. Or more than they joked about most things.

Eventually, he dubbed the screening room Room A, and the memorabilia room Room B. But matters got tricky when his wife kept leaving the frame. At first he put it down to her not knowing where her mark was.

When he expected to see an image of her beside him as he ran his latest masterwork, he'd notice instead that she was a good four or five feet to his right and his arm was around nothing but air. Maybe he was watching too much film, and a distortion element had affected his ability to evaluate properly. He took a few days off from his screening. But when he returned, late one night, overrun with anxiety—he hated to be away from what he considered his life's work—there was no mistaking that his wife was not in the frames, at all, of any of his recent footage. He went back to some of his earlier works, which he regarded as rough-hewn but not without promise, possessing, he believed, a certain intensity, if not, exactly, charm.

But she wasn't in those either. He was about to curse when he heard what he thought was the sound of her shoe down the hall, in Room B. Naturally, he paused the film and walked to his other movie room as quickly as possible and threw open the door, just in time to see what looked like a flickering field of light atop one of his favorite posters from the Basil Rathbone Sherlock Holmes series, and his wife making her away across the composition, one of those strange-looking ducks trailing behind her.

Or so it seemed. He redoubled his screening efforts, and soon he was going from one room of the house to another—that's how much his core images had become distended—trying to round up the cinematic expressions of his wife so he could restore them to their proper works.

He had a large bag, and he'd do what he could to transfer what he saw on the walls into it and get everything back upstairs, to the screening room, so he could start the business of restoring his original films. When he finally thought he had everything reassembled, and one long epic on his hands, he sat back to enjoy what he hoped would be a successful screening, only to sense some light behind him, out in the street that led to the headlands where he had shot such memorable footage of the harbor master and the occasional rogue lobsterman. Peeking through the blinds, he saw his wife again, a softly shimmering glow coming from her.

He took two bags with him this time, and every time he had to do his round-ups beyond the walls of the house, but the frame just kept breaking down, and there was no tracking the other portions of it when they got into different time zones, as he suspected they had, once he started to see that he, too, was missing from the footage, far away from his marks.

There were a few scenes of him in the barn with the animals, where he had never actually been, but soon they too were missing, and then the barn itself, only swaths of blackness remaining.

It was a curious sensation, feeling like he'd been etched right into the film, unviewable if someone else did not come along to run him through a projector. This was simply not tenable.

It was not easy pulling himself through the nitrate, but his environment was more translucent during the day, and as he had told his wife—when she once asked him whether he preferred the afternoon to the evening—he loved her very much, this would eventually come to the fore, she would see. Questions, though, as he knew, had a tendency to produce answers to other questions that no one had ever asked aloud. He thought maybe he should have taught her more about the qualities of silent movies.

BYGONE FRIGATES

DOSS WASN'T SURE this latest book on tape was a great investment after all. It had a knack for coming on when he least wanted it to, such as when he was otherwise engaged in a different pursuit.

Like when he'd sit in front of his television with his video game console. These were not easy times. The video games, he had read, would provide a measure of relief. They could help with stress, someone informed him. This seemed to make sense. Doss no longer had chairs, and he had no lights, but the television worked, so far as he could tell, and that was discounting the times he had walked in front of it, during the day, when the sun was out, and he could look across the room at the television and see himself going past a backdrop of waves and what seemed to be early sailing vessels.

Doss figured he had probably walked in front of the television when a maritime program was on, but still, it was fun to think that maybe, without his knowing it—perhaps while he was asleep—he had come by another identity. Or an additional one. Sleep had also been problematic, but that night he opened the windows, regardless of the cold, and tried to imagine himself as a midshipman tied to the rigging of a frigate, for he had once read that this is how midshipmen were sometimes punished.

True, punishment was not ideal, but the midshipman scenario would make for a nice respite from his normal dreams, which had the tendency to feel quite real, and in which Doss discovered he still owned chairs and lights, and was blessed with a good deal more besides. He did not enjoy the contrast when he awoke.

His efforts to transport himself to some bygone frigate hadn't been working, so he returned to the video game console. It sputtered when he attempted to turn it on, loudly enough that his book on tape was roused to action. The tape recorder was very sensitive. Sometimes a footfall was enough to tamp the play button down.

"Probably the salt must have done it. The salt in the air. All of the salt in the air on this crisp morn, but paces from the sea..."

Doss liked the lilting quality in the reader's voice, which had a bit of an Irish brogue, but nothing so thick that you couldn't always discern, Doss concluded, what that voice was saying in its most mellifluous ways. Actually, Doss purchased his books on tape by that reader and that reader alone—a voice artist billed simply as Padraig. No last name, or maybe that was his last name. On account of his devotion to this one reader, Doss had a most varied collection of books on tape, one that made him appear a more versatile listener than he probably was.

As a measure of compensation, he owned but one video game, a hockey video game. That morning he left the windows open, thinking maybe the salt air would help him in his quest to serve a spell or two in the rigging, and then get on to better things while he slept. There had been problems, though, with the man Doss controlled in the video game. He had been less robust of late. Games, even at the lowest level, were hard to win. But on that day there was no fight whatsoever. Doss fiddled with the controller, but the hockey player inside the television, where the masts and spars and birds frequently wavered as Doss walked past, was having none of it. He skulked to the edge of the screen and hopped up on a table, the way one does at the doctor's office. He put his head in his hands, shook his head, and then threw up on the floor, the digitized vomit passing cleanly between his legs.

It was like that for a few more mornings yet. The man who had been the hockey player would leave the screen entirely, and Doss would watch as he went to his own home, which also lacked chairs and lights, but featured a television set, where the man who was a player controlled another man—a smaller one—who played hockey on his TV as well. There was little cheer to be found in this. Maybe people had been wrong about the salubrious effects of trying to put his mind to other things. When the hockey player's hockey player stopped playing for him, the fellow turned and looked at Doss, shrugged, and stepped out the side of the television, alighting on the floor with enough of a footfall to start the book on tape again.

"...where the acting lieutenant found himself alone, stripped, for the moment, of his command, haunted by questions of what if and what should have been, tempted to kick the next poor creature to cross his path, but knowing he would really be kicking himself..."

The little hockey player shrugged again and motioned toward the window, making a kicking motion, as though Doss was supposed to give him a whack with his foot and send him hurtling through the glass. But both of them knew, because of their recent experiences, that there was not a great deal of motivation in the room, and given that it was soon time for Doss to start crying—as he normally did just before midday—the little hockey player shrugged a final time and headed out of the bedroom, head and shoulders slumped, digitized stick trailing behind him.

Doss watched through the window as the wind made off with his erstwhile companion, knowing that his video game console was now entirely useless. He gave it a sharp rap anyway, or as sharp a rap as he could muster, with his pen, which had been otherwise engaged writing in the latest notebook, since he believed—or hoped—that in writing out everything that had happened to him, back when he had chairs and lights, maybe he could understand why someone would wish to create such a scenario, when such a scenario could be avoided. When there was ample room for chairs and lights, and so much more—like people, or, more to the point, one other person. The pen had much the same effect as a good footfall, and at least Doss was able to resume his latest book on tape.

"For such was the acting lieutenant's nature, a nature he had worked to understand, and felt it necessary to do so, if he was to go forward in life, if not, necessarily, the King's royal navy. For just as his crew had come to respect him more, his wife had come to respect him less, and even feared him, and now he found himself without ship or companion, with little hope of having either again if matters did not change dramatically, both in the war against France and in the war of attrition that a heart is often forced to undertake. He lived in hope of coming upon an opportunity to…"

Doss wondered if he was that particular reader's biggest fan, or if readers of books on tape generated significant audiences because of the style in which they read, more so than what was portrayed, at the level of language, in the text at hand.

But given that it was now past midday and the crying had been got out of the way and the affair with the video game console concluded, it was time for an hour or so in the tub, a method of treatment which had also been suggested as a way to relax, to recharge, to reflect, maybe even to believe that he was not deserving of what had happened and that things might improve one day, which everyone had promised him.

Granted, he had promised them that things would not improve, ever, pointing out that, in these matters, one promise simply canceled out another, and that this could be someone's life. Someone could have a life like this. Things didn't always have to right themselves.

He had fielded a number of phone calls on this subject before the phone had stopped working and he had pitched it out into the yard through the window, the same window that the little hockey man had wanted to be kicked through. People wanted clarity from him. He was sorry that everyone was upset. He was sorry that he could not make them less upset by offering anything in terms of analysis or a far-flung theory.

One man had said he was not used to not knowing things, and so this was proving most challenging—most challenging—for him. In the abstract, Doss sympathized, and said he wished there was something he could do. This was well before he ever wondered if he had an alternate identity, or an additional one, where he had been to sea and presumably had experiences, life-changing experiences, that made him wiser, gave him a sagacity beyond that owed to his thirty-odd years of existence upon the land.

Doss wanted to help this man. He asked what he could do. The man said he could talk. So Doss did, trying to come up with answers, hoping that if he said enough words he might hit upon a combo that had some merit, some veracity. The man, meanwhile, sat in silence, listening, waiting, hoping, until it was clear that a winning combo was not forthcoming and that all of this was very draining, very depressing, and the man had to go. He didn't call much after that, but no one did. Doss understood.

The porcelain of the tub always felt cold. Doss put both of his legs over the side, on the right, and stared at his shoelaces, wondering if maybe he could learn, someday, if things ever improved and he became better at leisurely pursuits, how to tie a spliced sheet bend knot, or a Spanish bowline. Truthfully, though, Doss had entered a phase of his life where knots frightened him, just as the prospects of driving a car frightened him, the latter more than the former. Knots were tricky; the situation he imagined in the car, easy and inevitable. Sliding into the tub, sans water, to rest his eyes for a few moments in the darkness, typically had the effect of a footfall, and the sound of Doss's favorite book-on-tape reader would waft into the bathroom, which no longer had a door, as he had removed all the doors and stacked them in the backyard, now that doors tended to frighten him as well.

"...redeem himself, or, that failing, to finally make his departure away from the land that he had once viewed as his home, an inviolable space that had proven not so, and yet challenged him in ways, as a man, as a person, as a soul that drifted amongst other souls, eyeless, sightless, but still yearning for growth, or to be hammered into something else. There was the question of the submersible. Was it ready for launch? Dare he set about making his way to the ridge and the ravine, hoping that the knowledge he discovered in the latter would allow him and his craft to withstand the pressures of the former? Because what one has to ask oneself..."

But Doss was through with his latest book on tape for this latest day. Normally he would flop out of the tub, and the sound was enough to quiet the tape recorder. He'd walk to the back window, where the hockey man had stood, awaiting the kick that never came, and look at the pile of doors he had made behind the house that he would soon be departing, wondering if he'd climb atop the stack and clear the top of the fence in a submersible of his own that he felt fairly certain no one else could see, discounting the creatures of the ravine.

DUNES UNDER SAND

FIRST, COME UP WITH a term—the catchall, the crystallizer. The grand summarizer that you can say to the people who've ridden along, more or less, throughout the ordeal, and they will know, for all time, to what you are referring. You've already got a mess of these terms for other life events, and this one is going to need one, if anything else ever did.

Let's see. The Coalescent Moment. No. The Cumulative Moment. The Shoaling Moment. Nope. Leave it for now. It'll come.

But you know what they will say. What they will all say. The people who slagged you off, who said you were...a render. You rend. You're a buster-aparter. But that was early days. Before more—material—began to filter in. You know what that once-upon-a-time faction will say now. Just like you know what the ones who gave you more backing will say. Everyone got to the same point. Took a while though, didn't it? Or not so long? How do you measure something like that? We'll leave it for now. What they all will say—as though you needed me to tell you, but

still, that's how you are, a re-peruser: the past is the past
is the past is the past is the past is the past is the present—
ha, just fooling—is the past is the past. Leave it. Leave it
there. The past is the past is the past is the past—hearing
us now?—is the past is the past is the past. Leave—

*Okay. Okay. But it's not quite that simple. Listen to me.
Talking like I'm a state, a point on a map, a "here" you go
to. Not for your holidays. Don't come this way for your winter
break, or that late August, what do the kids call it now—vacay.
But what about "Strawberry Fields Forever." The Beatles. John
Lennon. Can you name a more futuristic song? But they did
it in the present, and it's about the past. John Lennon. Smart
guy. People would agree. The past didn't go anywhere for him.
Didn't slow him down. Does anyone see me slowing down?*

Yes. In a sense. You know this. You know you are
winding down. Or that you could be. You wished you
weren't when you met the woman on the plane. Not that
you really met her. Although, one could say—as you
have, of course—that you more than met her. But it's not
her time yet. She is still in our future, which is measured
in paper. You had that professor, way back. And he said
something like, people speed up when they know they
are near their end, if their body or mind is fully opera-
tional, and what they do in life centers on the one that
is still going strong. He cited Keats or some poet you
had never heard of. You didn't have to take that class,
of course. You just did. Funny what you remember. So
does that explain your pace, your rampancy? Who knew
you could do so much in so little time? Bet you wish you
knew that before, eh?

(..)

I see you're going to mull that for a bit. I'll continue. You thought no one could work like you worked. And all of that getting nowhere. The lack of promotions. Getting laid off. Taking that next job. So beneath you. Laid off from that, too. All of that creativity, what you rightly— you were actually right—considered acumen. Being right can make matters worse though, can't it? Next came the yelling. God how you yelled. Screamed. And then, because you are not as bad as some people originally believed after the—what was it you termed it?—

The Exodus Moment.

No. There was something else.

The TEM. I made an acronym. But then there were two "the"s.

Right. Thus my confusion. And then, after the yelling, because, as I was saying, you were not as bad as some people originally stated after she left, you expressed your concern to this individual that you were going to hell because of the way you treated her. So there was some conscience in you. Or rather, some dim awareness. But that didn't stop the yelling. And it didn't stop her from saying the situation was complicated, the yelling was fine, she knew it was not about her, or a comment upon her. Carry on. So you did. But what I tried to tell you, although you were not ready to hear it—

Cut me a break. There's a time factor here.

Even for you?

Even for me.

But what I tried to tell you then, and which I will try to retell you now—consider it a refresher—is that as bad as you were, as much as you put on yourself after, there was a lot you were each doing to each other. Awful though you were. I get the occasional email from her conscience. We're old rugby mates. He slacks off a lot. His whole family was like that. But he'll get around to putting in a decent day's effort at some point. Might take a decade. He's union.

Yes, yes, yes. The gaslighting. Gaslight: 1944 film with Ingrid Bergman and Charles Boyer. Latter tries to drive the former out of her mind through deft passive-aggressive manipulation that makes the victim call reality into question, and what is actually, creditably happening, and normal. There is also a 1938 film version. Us in the car. Me: "Do you want to get a coffee?" Silence. "Do you want to get a coffee?" Silence. "Do you want to get a coffee?" Silence. "Do you want to get a coffee?" Her: "What?" Have that happen a hundred times— or four—the yelling starts. Nice weather we're having, right? Nice weather we're having, right? Three more times. Nothing. Fat tourist walks by. Nice weather we're having, right? "Oh, yes, it's beautiful" comes the answer, straight away. "Want to get a coffee?" Silence. Then yelling. Who could be like that? No one? Okay. No one. So what, then? Me with my stuff, her with hers. There was only one bad guy, though.

Ah, yes, your skill set. I'm sorry. That still cracks me up.

What the fuck?

I'm sorry. When she left you, in the middle of the night, and you showed up at that house that you chose together and everything was gone—and the night before, she had called your mother, got you pizza, said she loved you— and those dust bunnies looked up at you, when you got there, like, "Sorry, mister, it's just us, sorry, this sucks for you, sorry," I wasn't expecting that there'd be five weeks of silence, not a word, save that man who looked like the postman from *Mr. Roger's Neighborhood*—

Mr. McFeely.

Mr. McFeely, with his divorce papers, and then you had those emails back and forth, after you'd written her how many words of contrition, where you said you'd do anything for the marriage—

At that point it was about 200,000. You know that. Why are you doing this?

I want to make sure you know it. And more than know it. What was I telling you about beaches?

No. I was telling you. That just because you see a dune, and it's all, look at me, I'm a dune, I'm a little sandy hill, see? Doesn't mean that when you come across a flat part of beach, of sand, that there's not some massive dune below, like it's upside down, and it can be never-ending, and tumescent, as far as inverted dunes go, and those are the dunes you have to watch out for. Because if that's the kind of dune you see when you go to the beach, you know just how hard it is for that clump of sand to explain what it's got going on under it. Hence all those iPod songs, probably. Wasn't just the beat after all. The Who's "I Can't Explain," the Strokes' "Hard to Explain." My soundtrack to my inability to understand.

Do you want me to put this on the progress side of the ledger?

Do what you want.

Check. But even I, having known you, in some regards, longer than you've known you—do you see what I did there?—did not expect her to see you, for all of those hours, insisting on holding you, kissing you, touching you, and telling you what she told you. That after she left, she

had a protective escort into work because you were primed
to go on a killing spree, starting in the East, where she was,
and then heading to Washington, D.C, to take out her parents, and then on to Seattle to get her friend, and finally to
England to take out her sister. You don't have a car. So you
would have needed a Zip Car, naturally. And killing sprees,
my friend, are not your skill set. And this would have been
one epic, efficacious killing spree. That was why I laughed.
I also figured you'd have one of those bright yellow Zip
Cars and it'd look a little bit like you were in some modern,
violent, post-relationship version of *Herbie.*

That is pretty funny. But I think I am going to throw up now.
I will wait the usual amount of time.

**(Interlude: 2 mins, 47 secs, approximately, in which
eighty-two children will be born in the United States,
thirty-five people will die—in the literal sense—and
one can vomit, sit on the ground by the bowl, rub
one's face, sigh, flush, sigh, flush again, turn on the
tap and splash water over one's temples, and take a
slow walk, covering five yards, back to the bed.)**

Ready?
*Yep. I want to get through this part. It's not why I'm here
this time, so quickly: jump cut to a courthouse, two lawyers and
one father to my none, I'm dispossessed of the dream house I
found in the dream town where we spent so much time, where
I need to get back to, and why I am doing the whole rampancy
thing—hooray for Keats, I guess, even though he croaked like
he did (I looked it up). Judge tells me I'm fucked, basically, ain't
no way you're staying on the deed, you don't pay the mortgage,*

sends us out to the rotunda to negotiate, I weep in front of two lawyers and this is what I hear from the person who, when last I saw her, had her tongue in my mouth: "You almost killed me." Dead serious. How? Renal failure? AIDS? A loosened car tire? Which the first husband actually did. Came off, too, when she was driving. Slept with a rolling pin in her bed after that. Never stopped talking to him, though. I was probably a four on the one-to-ten scale of evil, when she left and I talked to those dust bunnies, but—lots of cooks in the kitchen, and I had clearly advanced to a ten. No more her, no more house, no more town. I went up there anyway. Two-foot Christmas tree—one of those sorts you keep outside and replant in the spring—had been taken out of the garage, where it had been living out its first—and, as it turned out—final, winter. She put it in front of the door. Left it there. Turned orange, House for Sale, open houses. The orange tree remained, the plucky vermillion tree of the I'll-trade-you-my-heart-for-a-Zip-Car house.

That was odd. Hard to explain. Sorry.

Talking to people. Talking to so many people. The latest attempt to say, in essence, "Do you understand?" The search for that elusive yes. Because if someone else did, maybe they could tell me. They'd be wise. They'd be wiser than anyone I know.

Hey.

We belong to the same fraction.

Mmmmm.

The hunt for shovels, the special make, with the edges that keep going out and out and extending until that thing that just needs to be found is finally hit upon. "Come on, let's get us down to the beach, dig up some flat ground! Aha! See? One of them inverted dunes. Told you. Something was there. Now: who can explain?" Some dick will say, hey, that's not just sand and an

*inverted dune, that's a dune in you—is this sand or blood or sea
or mud—this is confusing, and I'd be like, yeah, I fucking said
it was, that's why we brought the special kind of shovels.*

Some people never pay attention.

I'm going to do it now. My thing.

Good for you. That's why you're here. You always do
the recap before the next part. Wise. Nothing wrong with
reviewing. Think of all the times that reviewing led to
learning something new: same bit of game film, but new
stuff. And now you're on your own. Your part alone. The
"raw take," before our next—what do the kids say?—convo.
Perhaps not in the bed next time? Definitely not in a car.
Still not ready for the car. Too much temptation. Greet-
ings wall of bridge overpass. Introductions best avoided.
The floor is yours, and yours alone, sir. Good luck.

**(Interlude: 13 seconds. The time it takes for someone/
something to say that this page is now like a stage,
akin to the one that Linus walks out on in that Charlie
Brown Christmas special to make his little speech.)**

*The bigger exodus. The BE? No. No being. Hamlet scene?
Hamlet riff? No. My riff. She: East Coast: no. West Coast. Yes.
To family there. I go. Not in a Zip Car. Never would have made
it. Friend's frequent flyer miles. Go, they say. Go. Really. Go. I
know how much you—*

Yep. True. I know how much too.

*The flight. Awake. Like a vampire during the day. Only
Dracula made the bed. It's in the book. Fun fact. Anecdote.
What's the difference? Which would love fall under? Maybe
impression? Maybe all three. Expecting to be turned away. Re-*

buffed. Vigorously? How else can one be rebuffed? Probably someone else will do it. On the front lawn. Always picture it happening on the lawn. Only ever thought of it two weeks ago for the first time. Other first times. First meeting outside a subway stop. Got there first. Struck poses. Hoped to be caught in the one with hands clasped behind back, like a captain on his quarterdeck. Impressive. Confident. Caught scratching behind my ear instead. Always the way. Thought that was the last chance to get that right. Early on. Third date. Just knew. Knew like I had never known anything else before about someone else. Chances to practice the pose again. In future. In theory. Now. Stop. Not what this part is about.

Other firsts. First kiss. Inside a subway station. Second date. Her move. Clearly not her standard operating procedure. She felt it too. So certain once, so confused later. So contradictory now. First time I cried in front of her. First time she cried in front of me. First time I made her cry in front of me. First time I knew she was off crying somewhere else because of me. All the times I cried after she was gone that she never knew about.

Chased off the lawn by someone else. The fable of the blind pig and the acorn. Pig surely viewed acorn more favorably than I did that aunt. Chaos. Leave. Will call the cops. After everything you did to her. Etcetera. I wanted to say it. Do you understand? The dune above ground. That is what I did. The dune below ground. There are dunes below ground. Her part. And what I feel. The dune in me. That everyone was confused about. Was it sand? Was it blood? Was it sea? Was it edible? What about the special shovels? Do you understand?

Probably would not have. Understood the phone, though. Started dialing. A few hours to kill. Red-eye flight. What fun. Go to a ballgame. Let's check out their local nine. Life begins here. Anew. At the old ballpark. Try to get into the spirit. Buy a hot dog. Buy a beer. Stare at the hot dog. Stare at the beer. Drop the hot dog into the beer. Start stirring. Want to get in the beer. Won't fit. Drop it. Slosh. Fat man with his own beers oohs and says, "Shit."

No. That is to come. Bathroom stall. A Wendy's. What's the pain in the face? Like being stabbed. Pain in the back of the neck. Chest. Tight. Feels like being in a duck press. Any juices? Yep. Here they come. Wake up in them. How long asleep? Do you call that sleeping? Probably not. Face. Floor. Tile indentations. Cheeks wet. Vomit. Odor. Hand in pants. Not supposed to shit yourself in your thirties. Me. The would-be Zip Car marauder. Leaving a trail of slime. Follow the stench. Not my skill set, clearly. As anyone who knew me would know. Except the person who once knew me best.

Middle seat on the plane. Of course. In the airport bathroom mirror, broken blood vessels. Eyes. Cheeks. Forehead. Nose. Even chin. The power of the wretch. Stroke residue. Never liked the idea of strokes, but the phrase "stroking out" always had appeal. Curious.

Hipster has the window. Of course. Little beard. Reading a big book. Suitably abstruse. It's more for someone to see and less for him to read. Fool. Fraud. Fucker. Takes off his shoes. Hipster foot smell. Not my place to complain, all things considered. Hand to mouth. Drool. Negotiations a few rows forward. Someone wants to trade seats to sit with their child. Deal is made. Everyone is pleased. Attractive late-twenties woman does not know what is waiting for her. Sits down. Smiles. Hipster lifts book cover in the air. Behold. My abstruse book. Sees me again. Slams down armrest. Percussive. I watch. Woman watches. Bang. Then he slams it again. Just to make sure. Turn to my left. Armrest is up. Woman looks at it. I feel my mouth.

"If either of you guys need to get up to use the bathroom and I'm asleep, just wake me up. No big deal."

Hipster flashes book again. Scowls at me. I don't have a book. Never slept before in front of strangers. Pondering this as serving cart comes around. Flight attendant talking to old woman ten rows up. Do you understand? Do you understand? Do you understand? I laugh. Can't even tell who is saying it. Alcohol is extra. The gist. Do you understand? It ain't free. Seat in front of me goes back. Knees crunched. Dehydrated. What does it mean when you are glad you vomited because it'll be harder to start crying? Decide to ask hipster. He's asleep. Think about waking him up. Mister. Mister. I could use your help with a question, and a walk on the wing would do me some good. If you don't mind.

And then there it is. Head on my shoulder. Wake her? Shift? Leave it there. The blackness again. For how long? Can do the math. This time. Six hours. Head on top of head. Eyes so close lashes almost touch. Awake again.

"Hi."

"Hi."

Help get the bag down. A kiss on the cheek. "Good luck."

Didn't even know her name. Lots of things I did not know. Some new ones I have learned lately:

You can pace in the shower. Two steps in each direction.

Anything you can do once can be done again. In theory.

It is possible that I will sleep on a plane again.

a. That is both simple and

b. complicated. Like the difference between the dunes people point to and the dunes that alter their shapes inside of you while the twat beside you snores.

GAS GIANTS

THE LIGHTS IN THE SKYSCRAPERS at night were a poor substitute for the constellations. He tried to appreciate them anyway. Sometimes he got on his back or stood under a bridge and looked up through the grating, trying to get a new angle on the buildings overhead. This was quite a bit different, though, from standing on what were known as the headlands of the small coastal town where he had once lived. There, the constellations were irrefutable. You didn't need to try and get an angle to better see Cetus as Cetus, Cancer as Cancer. It was different in the city, because some people worked late, leaving their lights on, but if a coworker a few offices down checked out for the night, you naturally lost a portion of whatever constellation you were trying to imagine out of lights. True, it was exciting at first, when there would be a fire alarm and the lights would flash, but he knew that constellations did not normally behave this way, and they had never conducted themselves in such a fashion when he stood on the headlands overlooking the small coastal town, wondering if it was possible to jump from the cliff and hit the water without bouncing off the rocks in between. It was an especially sloping cliff, and that was probably why headlands was the preferred term.

"Are you a squatter," the girl—maybe she was a woman—asked. Her eyes were wide, but her mouth barely seemed to move as she spoke. Her chin was tapered but not pointed. More like the bottom of a U, he thought. He felt he should have been scared. Anxious, at the very least. Consumed by plans of flight. There was no door to the outside up here. So, what then? A bodily launch through the window? Splashy. The glass was coated in salt, a product of small coastal towns. He reckoned he used to eat a goodly amount of salt just by breathing in the town. He used a grease pencil at night for entertainment, tracing the shapes made by the salt crystal in the glass.

The moonlight was a serviceable guide, and he dared not put on the actual light. The woman who had been his wife would notice a spike in the bill, even if it were just pennies. Probably. Then again, he thought she would have noticed him by now. Despite the reports he had gotten—courtesy of his memories—it stood to reason that if he was by the sea—and that was undeniable—she was likely in a drier climate. Maybe a desert one. In truth, he never expected to get this far, assuming apprehension would have followed shortly after he tried the alarm in the middle of the night.

The constellations in the buildings back in the city had all gone dark. No one worked overtime anymore, and so he had returned to the house that had once been his, and which was now no one's. He was worried that the alarm code would be different, and the lock as well, but in he went, easy peasy, with the same old key, using the same old security code. The code had been his idea. "You could take all the money out of my account if you found my card and you had a sexual mind," he had remarked. The woman who had been his wife laughed. He was suspicious. "Well, you know how someone counts down to a race with one, two, three, go! All my codes are one, two, sixty-nine. Get it?" More laughter. Seems real enough, he thought then, and later, after she had gone, fostering more confusion in the process. And that was right near the end. Legit laughter at the end. You'd think it would definitely had to have been less honest. He tried to think and make it so. But no matter how often he tried—whether he was standing on the headlands, pondering if he could hit the water without bouncing, or on his back under a bridge staring up at a mutilated version of Cancer in the side of a skyscraper, or sitting in the woods near the small coastal town with a notebook beside him, opened to the letter he had drafted seventeen times over, waiting for the sound of the next train, the sound of his courage (he imagined it was probably something like a high-pitched whistle that blew, like a streamlined, audible laser, in your ears), or, eventually, standing in front of the woman who had chanced upon him in the house that had once been his, the woman who may have been a child, with the tapered chin and the alert eyes and the barely moving mouth—he could not get himself to think otherwise. "Yes, definitely legit," he concluded again and crawled to the window in the darkness, and waited for some night clouds to pass before the moonlight came streaming in once again. The grease pencil was under his foot. He had gone back and forth on whether it was better to leave his shoes on, in case he had to flee, or if a silent footfall would prove a most capable preventive. He'd made the decision to keep one on and one off. He flipped the grease pencil up to his hand. Legit, he wrote on the window, but he did not have a name for this particular constellation.

It did not feel right, that first night, to sleep in the bed. He was surprised it was still there. He smelled it. Seemed to be the same. He put an edge of the comforter into his mouth. Could have been indicative of her; it was tough to tell. He tried the pillow. Ah—the salt. Different salt. That was her. The times she had cried, at volumes so low he began to think there was a chance he had extraordinary hearing abilities. Maybe he was like a dog. So he stood on the headlands and looked for Canis Major, but he never did spot it. Perhaps that part of the world was only turned to certain constellations, regardless of the time of year. He resolved to look into the matter further, but not while listening to the sounds made by the woman who had been his wife. They tended to take up the bulk of his concentration. Creative thinking was of the essence. Why did she behave that way, with all of those emissions? What was it about her past that made her so just now? When he began to wonder if the way she was now was because of the way he had become, he redoubled his efforts. Her parents probably had something to do with it. Her diet. Not enough cool, clear, purgative evenings out on the headlands, overlooking the small coastal town, making educated deductions about where some constellations went hiding when you could no longer see them, and if you could hit the water, were you of a mind, without bouncing off the sloping cliff wall first. "Can I come with you?" she asked. "Where do you go? Your hair. There's always so much salt in it. Caked with salt. It gets on the pillow. And up into my nose, and in my ears, and in my eyes." This seemed reasonable to him. "So it has to come out, you're saying? A mere bodily process? Healthy, even?" It was in these moments that he was certain, thanks to his extraordinary hearing, that the crying started, and while he tried to accept her explanations, there was no denying that salt, pillows, bodily processes, and the darkened corners of rooms—and the conversations whispered from one side to the other—made for tricky business. In the dark, on the headlands, he reached into the bucket of stones he always took with him and tossed a piece of shale seaward, waiting for the plinking sound of something small entering something large. But the stone would always hit stone first, and he was never sure, despite his extraordinary hearing, if any of the stones in his bucket ever made it to the water, into something bigger. So he gathered a sandwich bag of pebbles and waited until it was as late as he thought it had ever been, like the universe had gone beyond itself and found an extra second to add on to the evening, a second it had spent years and years formulating, scrimping and saving on time when no one could possibly have been looking. And in that second, he threw a handful of pebbles at the bed. Nothing. Not a sound. Not stone on stone, stone on water, or stone on flesh. Not even stone on air.

The first portion of the first night he spent under the bed. Were someone to enter the room, he felt there was a decent chance he would remain undetected—after all, it

seemed like a cliché, these days, to look under the bed—
although it would be tough to secure his freedom, were he
located in situ. But he grew restless, so he tried the closet
instead. It was large enough that one—particularly if one
were fanciful—could view it as a bedroom, and deciding
to view it as such, he resolved to sleep in a corner of it and
leave the rest free for other matters. Like pacing, which he
accomplished by rolling from one side to the other. But it
was too dark in the closet, and he missed having the windows and the salt crystals close by, so in the end he opted
for the clawfoot tub. The moonlight streamed through
the bathroom window and lit up the salt in the glass, and
it was difficult not to imagine he was sleeping underwa-
ter, in the ocean. To enhance the effect he turned on the
water whenever he woke up, so that it gathered around
him. He was wet when he saw her, not having accounted
for open houses and the real estate business. "Are you a
squatter?" It seemed like she had asked the question several times, but her tone was so level that he thought it likely
he had imagined the repetitions, if not the whole encounter. Never had there been such equanimity of voice, he
was certain. Just like he had been certain that the universe
had created that extra second so he could make sure he
had no wife anymore. Surety. You had to be grateful for
surety. It was cleansing. Something, he concluded, that
would get the salt out of your hair, so to speak, after so
many nights on the headlands, overlooking a small coastal town, throwing rocks down to the ocean. He shook
his head and more salt tumbled onto his shoulders. There
was probably quite a bit at the bottom of the tub, too.
Like sediment, or bath salts. He wasn't really sure what

they were for. He pointed to the bathroom. "No. I used
to live here. I've also lived under the bed, in the closet,
and in the tub. Briefly. Or for a long time. It is hard to
tell. Things have a way of running together. Life tends
to get a bit…estuarial." She only stared at him. Not with
alarm, not with anger, not with affection. "One, two,
sixty-nine?" he offered.

His manner of discovery came to be thought of as romantic. She had claimed as much all along, but that seemed
difficult to believe, for him, anyway. Hoses were installed
around every side of the house, and he never did enter it
again before dousing his hair thoroughly and watching
the salt run out on the ground. Some squirrels acquired a
taste for the stuff, and while at first he was put off by the
sight of them licking the ground so rapaciously, he became
accustomed to it, and even welcomed them, just as he welcomed the sight of her on the headlands with him during
the day, pitching stones down toward the sea and hearing
the plink that had been so rare—so rare as to be what he
considered his mind's version of a rumor—in past times.
He dared not ask her what she knew about the universe's
ability to manufacture, by hook or crook, the occasional
extra second, which it stuck way back at the end of the
night, when you lost any sense of whether the night was
still the night or else the morning, or if there was some
region between both where so many things were planted,
and so much happened, without any solid ground at all.
The closet astronomer in him—he liked the pun—wondered if that second was like being on, or in, one of the gas
giants. That was what the books called them: Jupiter, Sat-
urn. Uranus, Neptune. Maybe that was why there'd been

no sound—for he had the most extraordinary hearing—when he lobbed that fistful of pebbles in the direction of the woman who had been his wife. He sat in the corner, in the dark, with another sandwich bag of pebbles. He had double-bagged this one to make sure nothing went awry. And he had given his hair a most thorough dousing to ensure that the salt in the house was no more than the salt in the windows, in crystal form, which still inspired him to trace the shape of constellations, and write, on occasion, the word legit. He gave a mighty heave and waited for the report. It did not take long.

"What are you doing now? Are you coming to bed or not? Do you know how late it is?" He paused. This might have been a loaded question. "Is it very late?" "Of course. It's almost morning. Now get your ass over here. Did you wash your head?" "I did. Many times." He paused again. "Do you want to do the alarm code thing? I could say the numbers first, like we're starting a race." "Just hold me." He took a quick peek under the bed, but it was too dark to see anything, so he kicked some of the stray pebbles away instead, letting out his breath when he heard them hit the wall.

POTLATCH

SORRY, PRINTER—I have asked a lot of you over these six months, printing out, as you know, over two million words, which I have sent, in effect, to someone who might as well be a ghost, who could be a ghost, as you suggested one evening, during one of our fanciful evenings, as you hummed like you do in the corner and I had yet another sip of the latest malted beverage, one of the kind I pour some coffee or tea into so as to stay awake a little longer, because we can't keep going to bed every night at seven o'clock, given that it leads to getting up at three in the morning, a bad time to start one's day when one cannot handle a normal full day, let alone a long day. It likely will not comfort you to know that more strenuous work is just around the corner. The final push. And though you sometimes shoot out one blank page after another for fifty pages, and I have to "cancel job," and shut you down, and start all over again—ah, what a metaphor, considering my present situation, but a taxing one, since I can only restart you—I know you mean well and are not plotting against

me. Know that I have done what you asked and made in-
quiries to the microwave. The one that works. Not the
one built into the cupboard (the slag) that I have filled
with books and Cadbury Eggs from years ago, from the
Better Times. (Cadbury Eggs refuse to go bad; and so hail
to you, Cadbury Eggs, hail to you and your fealty.) I think
she's up for it, mate. Will fill you in later. Meanwhile: keep
on churning. And yes, the curb. I am sorry you learned of
the curb in the manner you did. That was not my inten-
tion. My plan was to level with you. But you know how it
can be when one has had too much of the malted and the
blubbering turns to speechmaking in a soft, faintly Brit-
ish accent, in that quarter of an hour before passing out,
when life feels that it might be livable again, before the
morning comes to swat that idea away. So you know that
I will be putting you out again soon for the men to take.
For someone to take. No last-second change of heart this
time. You could well fare better elsewhere. Want to think
of it as a potlatch? A giving away of one's goods so that
others might enjoy them better. Because let's face it—so
long as you're here with me, I'm only going to keep trying,
even if the letters I write to her never get sent and become,
in a way, letters to me, saying things I already know a million times over, but which I feel like no one else has ever
known. Certainly not her. The lawyers? Of course not.
But potlatch. Please. View it that way. If she's game, I will
send you on your journey with the microwave, because
it's hard to feel like one deserves hot foodstuffs when one
gets to this particular circle of the abyss, with no further
ledges. It's like standing in the infinite darkness on the
last bench there ever was, with no ground below, no more

levels, just blackness. Think of the future I may well be ceding you. Do you offer the same to me? Of course not. So remember that on your next stop, and reflect back on me, if not kindly, then as someone who challenged you to be at your best, to test the range of your limits, to go beyond what might have been your limits, even. Plus: there's always blood, isn't there? There's always blood. Different color, same idea.

Colin Fleming writes for *The Atlantic*, *Vanity Fair*, *JazzTimes*, *Sports Illustrated*, *The New Criterion*, *Rolling Stone*, and *The Boston Globe*. His fiction appears in the *VQR*, *Boulevard*, *Black Clock*, *Post Road*, *The Cincinnati Review*, *AGNI*, and *The Massachusetts Review*. He is a regular contributor to NPR's Weekend Edition and Ireland's Tom Dunne Show.